KENSY
AND MAX
— UNDERCOVER —

D1411019

Kensy and Max Books

Kensy and Max: Breaking News
Kensy and Max: Disappearing Act
Kensy and Max: Undercover
Kensy and Max: Out of Sight

Jacqueline Harvey

KENSY AND MAX

== UNDERCOVER ==

Kane Miller
A DIVISION OF EDC PUBLISHING

First American Edition 2020
Kane Miller, A Division of EDC Publishing

First published Random House Australia in 2019,
Penguin Random House Australia Pty Ltd.
Copyright © Jacqueline Harvey 2019
The moral right of the author has been asserted.

All rights reserved. No part of this publication may be reproduced,
stored in a retrieval system, or transmitted, in any form or by any means,
electronic, mechanical, photocopying, recording or otherwise, without
the prior permission of the publisher and copyright owner.

For information contact:
Kane Miller, A Division of EDC Publishing
P.O. Box 470663
Tulsa, OK 74147-0663
www.kanemiller.com
www.edcpub.com
www.usbornebooksandmore.com

Library of Congress Control Number: 2019952228

Printed and bound in the United States of America
1 2 3 4 5 6 7 8 9 10
ISBN: 978-1-61067-994-7

For Ian, who makes things happen, and for Dot and Zoe, who are fabulous and some!

Map of
Sydney
Harbour

Dame
Spencer's
Terrace

Blues Pt. Rd.

Waiwera St.

PARK

The Chalmers
Residence

Luna
Park

Warung St.

McMahons Pt.
Wharf

Harbour
Bridge

Opera House

Circular
Quay

Royal Botanic
Gardens

Wentworth
Grammar

Art Gallery
of NSW

Dalefield Farm

Shed

Paddock

Caretaker's Cottage

Exeter Rd.

Cherry Tree Farm

Exeter General Store

Werai Rd.

Exeter Station

Map of
Cherry Tree
Farm

CAST OF CHARACTERS

The Grey household

Kensington Méribel Grey — Agent-in-training, 11-year-old twin to Max

Maxim Val d'Isère Grey — Agent-in-training, 11-year-old twin to Kensy

Anna Grey — Dormant agent PA S2694, Kensy and Max's mother

Edward Grey — Dormant agent PA S2658, Kensy and Max's father, eldest son of Dame Spencer

Fitzgerald Williams — PA S2660, Kensy and Max's manny, nephew of Dame Spencer

Song Li	PA U2613, butler
Sidney Li	PA U2614, Dame Spencer's butler in Wilton Crescent

Pharos

Dame Cordelia Spencer	Head of Pharos
Rupert Spencer	PA X2672, Dame Spencer's son
Magoo MacGregor	PA P2659, headmaster of Central London Free School
Romilly Vanden Boom	PA P2646, science teacher at Central London Free School
Monty Reffell	PA P2667, history teacher at Central London Free School
Autumn Lee	Agent-in-training
Carlos Rodriguez	Agent-in-training

Wentworth Grammar staff

Thaddeus Thacker	Headmaster
Stella Black	Assistant to the headmaster
Divorah Skidmore	Receptionist to the headmaster, choir stylist
Harriet Sparks	Choir manager
Mrs. Strump	Choir pianist
Jaco De Vere	Head cricket coach

Wentworth Grammar students

Curtis Pepper	Year Five student, neighbor
Donovan Chalmers	Year Six student, son of Dash and Tinsley
Ellery Chalmers	Year Five student, daughter of Dash and Tinsley
Dugald McCrae	Year Six student, talented tenor
Lucienne Russo	Year Six student, talented soprano

Other

Dash Chalmers	Owner of The Chalmers Corporation, father of Donovan and Ellery
Tinsley Chalmers	Wife of Dash, mother of Donovan and Ellery
Derek Grigsby	Shopkeeper
Rosa	Housekeeper to the Chalmers
Simone Stephenson	Stonehurst choir mistress
Lucy Dowsett	Executive assistant to Dash Chalmers
Nick	Cherry Tree Farm manager
George Kapalos	Investigative journalist
Hattie Pendleton	Central London Free School student

Case Note 17

Author: Fitzgerald Williams, Pharos Agent (PA) S2660

Subjects: Kensington Grey, PA A2713; Maxim Grey, PA A2714

Kensington and Maxim Grey were admitted as Pharos agents-in-training at the age of eleven years and one month.

FIELDWORK

On a recent school history tour to Rome, Kensington, Maxim and three of their friends and co-agents-in-training – Autumn Lee, Carlos Rodriguez and Misha Thornhill – were instrumental in solving two major interlinked crimes: the first being the opportunistic kidnapping of Nico Vitale, son of the prime minister of Italy; and the second, a plot holding the prime minister for ransom over the control of the wheat and pasta industry by the highly elusive crime syndicate known as the Diavolo.

Misha Thornhill had been tasked with befriending Lola Lemmler, a fellow student at Central London Free School, in order to gather intelligence on the girl's father (alias Steve Lemmler, real name Sergio Leonardi), a known kingpin of organized crime. Through the children's efforts, Sergio Leonardi was revealed as the head of the Diavolo, working alongside the president of Italy and a gang of thieves led by a woman disguising herself as a nun. The Diavolo is notorious for a wide range of criminal activities, including petty theft, extortion, money laundering and arms dealing. Their crimes and misdemeanors run to practically all areas of life in Italy.

The impromptu mission was sanctioned by Dame Cordelia Spencer while the children's teachers and agents – Monty Reffell, Romilly Vanden Boom, Elliot Frizzle and Lottie Ziegler – were also mobilized. The other agents-in-training on the trip were not involved and the civilian students among the group remained completely unaware of the events that unfolded. I was able to assist the children in the final phase of their assignment with the help of Lottie Ziegler and the twins' uncle, Rupert Spencer. Alessandro Grimaldi, head of the Italian secret service, was in charge of the arrests at Quirinal Palace, where the president of Italy and his associates were intercepted and taken into custody. Following the completion of their mission, Kensy, Max, Autumn, Carlos and Misha continued their school history tour.

SKILLS, STRENGTHS AND VULNERABILITIES

Maxim consistently astonishes his teachers with his photographic memory. While it was his ability to remember maps in exceptional detail that initially caught everyone's attention, Maxim's visual recall capabilities have excelled in all manner of situations. Meanwhile, Kensington has recently been honing her skills in robotics in addition to her interest in mechanical engineering. This has led to some surprising and slightly alarming inventions, which have proven both interesting and useful. Her knowledge of machinery was extremely helpful when the washing machine at Ponsonby Terrace recently broke down.

TRAINING

In the week before Christmas, Kensington and Maxim participated in intensive training exercises at Alexandria, the countryside headquarters of Pharos. During this time they were given instruction on tactical strategies via a range of stealth, combat and marksmanship activities. The children were trained in the use of firearms and other weaponry, such as crossbows and regular bows and arrows. Kensington and Maxim learned to drive with Esmerelda, the computerized vehicle responsible for teaching all Pharos agents. Despite both children displaying impressive skills, an unfortunate mishap rendered Esmerelda almost completely destroyed. The twins were lucky to survive the fiery incident.

The children have also continued developing their proficiency in code breaking and orienteering with Maxim emerging top of the class in both areas, although he tied with Autumn Lee in code breaking. Kensington's ability to pick locks is unsurpassed and her use of the regulation school hair clip to assist her in this area has been creative, to say the least.

Several new gadgets have been revealed to them, including the Blunderbus Bubble Gun, which was used to remarkable effect by Rupert Spencer during a car chase in Rome; lasso shoelaces, which both twins have access to; and poison-dart glasses currently being trialed by Maxim.

EMOTIONAL STATE

While Maxim has maintained a stable emotional state, it has become apparent that Kensington is struggling to deal with recent events. A sudden growth spurt is likely not helping either. She has been prone to outbursts and has fallen behind in some areas of her studies, which has landed her in a spot of bother with several of her teachers. One notable incident occurred in an art lesson, where Kensington absent-mindedly painted over a canvas that Elliot Frizzle was partway through completing for the London Landscape Prize. Despite Kensington's somewhat erratic behavior, both children have done a very good job of adapting to their new and unusual life and are keeping busy with school and training.

UPDATE ON THE DISAPPEARANCE OF ANNA AND EDWARD GREY

Anna and Edward Grey made contact with Kensington and Maxim in Rome, appearing briefly inside a confessional booth in St. Peter's Basilica. While it came as a shock to the children, they were both overjoyed and are still confident their parents will soon return. I plan to brief the twins more fully on their parents' self-directed mission to recover their maternal grandparents, who, while presumed dead in a botched robbery and subsequent fire in Paris 12 years ago, have recently been revealed to be alive. Kensington and Maxim have deduced considerable insights about this themselves. Having discussed the case with Anna and Edward, we have come to the conclusion that, rather than leave the children to speculate further and inadvertently say something they shouldn't, they must be privy to the information available. Anna and Edward have given consent to brief Cordelia as well, though the information is Status Grey, for her eyes only. The possibility of a mole within the organization remains high, and although Kensington is convinced it is Shugs, a gardener at Alexandria, I am not of the same opinion.

OTHER INFORMATION

Kensington and Maxim will continue to live at Ponsonby Terrace with Song and myself until their parents return and a decision is made as to whether they will remain as agents-in-training. Given their obvious skills and knowledge of Pharos, I believe it will be near impossible to convince them to give up their new life. I cannot imagine Maxim's knife-throwing prowess would be sought after in many vocations outside of the circus, and Kensington is proving herself to have excellent intuition, despite her impetuousness. The children have both expressed a great desire to continue with the family firm.

CHAPTER 1

IVZORGB YRGVH

Kensy measured the powder into the beaker, then added an extra spoonful for good luck. "What's next?" she asked, drumming her fingers on the lab bench. It hadn't escaped her notice that numerous pairs of students had already ignited their mixtures.

Autumn looked up from the sheet of paper, where she had been reading through each step of the experiment. "It says here that the powder has to go in there," she said, pointing to the small bowl filled with sand that had been soaked in lighter fluid.

Kensy picked up the beaker and tipped the mixture onto the granules.

"Now you can set it on fire," Autumn instructed.

"Well done, Max and Carlos, that's fantastic!" Mrs. Vanden Boom exclaimed from the other side of the room. She swiftly moved on to congratulate Inez and Yasmina.

Kensy glowered. She flicked on the lighter and thrust it into the bowl of powder. She and Autumn watched closely as it sizzled and flashed, the flames rising higher and higher.

"I don't think it's supposed to do that," Autumn said, anxiously glancing around at her classmates. Everyone else's flames had died down once the chemical reaction had transformed the powdered mixture into a charcoal snake. Theirs, however, was only intensifying.

Kensy gulped. "We need to put it out." She grabbed a small beaker of water and poured it over the bowl, which instantly exploded into a fireball. Kensy leapt backward just in time to avoid losing her eyebrows.

"Fire!" Inez shouted as the flames shot toward the ceiling.

Several of the children screamed.

Romilly Vanden Boom spun around from where she'd been running through the experiment for the third time with Dante and Sachin. "Good heavens! How on earth did that happen?" She sped to the front of the room, sidestepping the lab benches and launching herself at the fire blanket that was hanging from a hook.

By now the ceiling had begun to ignite. Max ran for the extinguisher and wrenched it from the wall while Mrs. Vanden Boom pulled the blanket from its pouch and hurtled back to the inferno. She threw it on the bowl just as Max pulled the pin and aimed the nozzle toward the burning ceiling. Thankfully, the flames were snuffed out in seconds and there were only a few scorch marks to show what could have been so much worse. But it was already too late. The fire alarm had been triggered.

"Oh no, this is bad." Kensy turned to

Autumn, biting her lip. "I didn't mean to. It was an accident."

Romilly sighed. "Right, everyone, walk sensibly to the front entrance – there's to be no running," she ordered.

Kensy and Autumn joined the rest of the students in the hallway, where the sirens were still blaring.

"What were you girls doing?" Mrs. Vanden Boom demanded when she caught up to the pair.

"It was my fault," Kensy said. "I think I might have added too much baking soda."

"Hmm, that shouldn't have turned your snake into a flamethrower. That doesn't make any sense at all," Romilly said, shaking her head. She ushered her class through reception and out onto the tiny patch of front lawn, where she began to count heads. Kensy and Autumn fell into line alongside the rest of the school population. "I want to see you in my office at lunchtime, Kensy. We need to t–"

"But, Mrs. Vanden Boom," Kensy interrupted, "I have to see Mr. Frizzle first, then I've got detention with Miss Witherbee."

Romilly frowned at the girl. "I'll send a message to the others. This is serious, Kensy. We've been back at school for almost six weeks and in that time you've deleted the programming for your robot, you almost lost a finger in a vat of acid and you just set fire to the lab – and that's only in your science lessons. I hear there have been other mishaps too. We need to have a chat to find out what's going on with you, okay?"

Kensy nodded, feeling sick to her stomach.

"My office in twenty," the woman said. "Downstairs."

There was much speculation among the student body about what had happened, with murmurs ranging from burned toast in the staff room to someone smoking in the bathroom, until Sachin set everyone straight, telling them loudly that Kensy was to blame. A blast of heat rose to the girl's cheeks.

"Good one, Kensy," Hattie Pendleton moaned. "We were in the middle of an exam. Now we'll have to stay in at lunchtime to finish it."

Kensy's eyes narrowed. "Oh, put a sock in it, Hattie," she snapped.

Her twin brother, Max, caught her gaze. "Don't worry," he mouthed, touching his left ear ever so quickly – their secret signal that everything would be all right. But, truthfully, he was worried about her. Kensy hadn't been herself since their trip to Rome. He'd tried talking to her, but she was either touchy or fobbed him off with a joke.

Monty Reffell emerged from the building last of all. He wore a bright-orange hard hat and matching hi-vis vest, which didn't go well with the rest of his outfit, given that he'd been teaching a lesson about World War II and was currently dressed as Winston Churchill, in a tweed suit and bow tie, complete with a pillow down his front for extra bulk.

"All clear," the man declared as the convoy of wailing fire engines pulled up to the gate.

Several firemen leapt out and ran to the front steps, where they were greeted by the headmaster.

"Sorry, chaps," Mr. MacGregor said. "One

of the children tried to burn down the science lab, though, fortunately, she didn't succeed." He looked at Kensy and gave her a wink, but the girl wasn't smiling.

Her brain was in overdrive. Seriously, she needed to get her head back in the game or there was no way she'd be passing her first Pharos review nor her fifth-grade exams.

CHAPTER 2

MVDH

Cordelia Spencer ended the call and stared vacantly at the opposite wall. When, finally, her eyes refocused, they fell upon the framed photograph on her desk of her late husband, Dominic. Cordelia still missed him every single day and could well do with a dose of his wisdom right now.

Faye Chalmers, Cordelia's oldest and dearest friend in the world, had just delivered some troubling news. The two had known each other since kindergarten, having grown up a street apart in a leafy suburb of Sydney's lower north shore. It was only when it came time to go to university that the pair went their separate ways. Cordelia took a scholarship at Oxford, and Faye attended Sydney University before completing a PhD at Harvard. It was fair to say that both women were trailblazers, far ahead of their time. Cordelia had gone on to run the *Beacon* and, of course, Pharos, which Faye knew nothing about; while Faye and her husband, Conrad, went from opening a small pharmacy in South Carolina to establishing one of the world's largest and most respected pharmaceutical companies, The Chalmers Corporation.

Despite being separated by the North Atlantic, Faye and Cordelia had kept in regular contact over the years, doing their best to catch up as often as their busy schedules allowed. Mostly, it was an odd birthday, anniversary or untimely funeral. Without fail, though, they spoke every fortnight, and during the previous two calls it was clear that Faye's son, Dash, and his wife, Tinsley, were having problems. Things had apparently worsened considerably, with Dash confiding in his parents that he thought Tinsley was planning to leave him and take the children with her – quite possibly overseas. Cordelia had always thought Tinsley a very level-headed woman and had been shocked by the news. It was a horrible situation and she felt desperately sorry for the poor children caught up in their parents' drama.

Faye and Conrad were stuck in the United States, unable to travel due to ill health while their son and his family lived in Sydney. Cordelia worried a family breakup might just push her friends over the edge. The pair had suffered enough with the sudden death of their daughter, Abigail. It had changed the course of all their lives, not least Cordelia's son Rupert, who had just become engaged to the young woman when tragedy struck.

Cordelia realized the eyes on the brass monkey paperweight on her desk had begun to glow. She'd been hoping to leave work early this afternoon, but apparently there was something that couldn't wait. She stood up and walked to the bookcase, pulling out her favorite copy of *Pride and Prejudice*. Silently, the cabinetry slid apart to reveal an elevator. Cordelia stepped inside, her thoughts still very much on Faye. If only she could keep an eye on things for her – but using Pharos resources for family affairs wasn't something she'd ever permitted and it wouldn't be appropriate now, not even for her best friend in the world.

CHAPTER 3

LKVM ULI YFHRMVHH

"I'll meet you at the front gate," Max called.

Kensy slammed her locker door and stalked down the corridor, her face a storm cloud.

"Yikes. Is she okay?" Carlos asked.

Max checked which books he needed to take home for the weekend and arranged them neatly in his bag. "I haven't talked to her since she had her meeting with Mrs. V.B., but I'm sure she'll be fine. There's just been a lot going on. See you tomorrow?"

"Yep, and maybe we can go to the Natural History Museum afterward," Carlos said excitedly, hitching his backpack higher on one shoulder. "I hear they have a new 'Life in the Dark' exhibit with all these cool bioluminescent sea creatures and nocturnal beasts — it might help with our science project."

Max relished having a friend who shared his love of facts. He'd never had that before. "Sounds good," he said, grinning. "See you then." Max hurried out of the school and looked around, but Kensy was nowhere to be seen. It was only when he crossed the street that he saw her perched on the low brick wall in front of an apartment building.

"Hey," he said, making sure to keep his distance.

Kensy jumped to the ground. "Hey yourself."

"That bad, huh?"

Kensy shrugged. "At least Mrs. Vanden Boom didn't attempt to kill me like somebody else is clearly trying to do."

"You still think someone's out to get us?" Max asked.

"Yes . . . no . . . oh, I don't know." Kensy

kicked at a pebble on the ground. "I just wish things would go back to the way they were before, but then I don't really want that at all because we wouldn't know Granny and Uncle Rupert and Song and everyone else."

Max gave her a reassuring smile. "I suppose being part of the world's most powerful spy agency has to come with a certain amount of risk attached. Kens, try not to worry so much. We couldn't be in safer hands."

"Don't be so sure, Max. Plus, aside from the whole life-threatening situation, I don't want to fail my first review – what would Granny and Fitz think? It'd be mortifying. How could I show my face at school again? It was almost easier before we spoke to Mum and Dad." Kensy stopped and looked at him. Max was struck by the emotion on her face. "Does that make me a bad person?"

"Of course not," Max said gently. "At least we now know for sure that they're alive and why they disappeared. Imagine if they find Mum's parents. How incredible would that be after all this time, after everything our family has been through?"

The twins resumed walking down the street, their schoolbag zippers jingling in the silence.

"Do you ever think about what they're like?" Kensy asked after a while. "Or what we'd call them? They're French, so probably *grand-mère* and *grand-père*, right?"

"I guess," Max said. "Remember those pictures of them in the newspaper we saw in the family crypt? I have that photograph of them imprinted on my mind – except, of course, they'll be older now."

The pair turned the corner and were surprised to see the shutters were up on Mrs. Grigsby's newsagency. The place had been boarded up as tight as Fort Knox ever since Wanda Grigsby and her son, Derek – along with two other elderly ladies, Esme Brightside and Ivy Daggett – had been arrested for stealing the Graff Peacock Brooch, estimated to be worth eighty million pounds, from the Tate Gallery. Kensy and Max had been instrumental in the gang's apprehension, but it was MI6 who took the credit. The sting had also led to the capture of the women's husbands, who had pulled off the largest diamond heist in British history a year before and were in hiding overseas.

"They couldn't be out of prison already, could they?" Max said.

"No way, it's been less than two months," Kensy said. "Someone else must have bought the shop. That's good. We can get treats on the way home again. I've got five pounds – what do you want?"

Kensy dumped her bag at the front door and Max followed her in. The place looked exactly the same but for a thick layer of dust and cobwebs spun into the corners. There was an acrid tang in the air too. The twins headed straight for the confectionary aisle. Max chose a chocolate-and-nut bar while Kensy grabbed a bag of red frogs for Song and a small bag of mixed sweets for herself. They walked to the counter, which was presently unattended. Kensy tapped the little bell.

"Comin'!" a familiar voice rang out from the back room.

The twins looked at one another. "Derek?"

they whispered in unison, and turned to find the fellow ambling toward them. He was wearing a gray beanie, Rolling Stones T-shirt and jeans that were riding lower than ever. His "jenius" tattoo was on full display on his left forearm.

"Hiya, kids," he said, a broad grin sweeping across his face. His gold tooth glinted under the fluorescent lights. "I can't tell you how good it is to see you two."

"We thought you were on holiday in the Caribbean," Max said, finding his voice.

"Oh." Derek frowned. "Yeah, that didn't quite work out."

"Did your mum go?" Kensy asked, glancing around the shop. There was no sign of the wretched woman and she couldn't hear any noises coming from the apartment upstairs.

"You kids don't read the papers, do you?" Derek said, resting his elbows on the countertop and leaning in toward them.

"Not much," Max mumbled, which wasn't true at all. He read the *Beacon* from cover to cover each morning before school. He'd always kept up with current affairs, but he particularly made an effort now that he was a Pharos agent-in-training and especially because one of the agency's primary methods of communication across the globe was through meticulously plotted advertisements, notices, puzzles and stories that were planted in the paper.

"That's good. It's just a load of old rubbish most of the time." Derek unwrapped a chocolate bar from the front counter and bit into it. "Me mum won't be back for ages. I'm gonna run the shop while she's away."

Kensy suppressed the smirk that was tickling her lips and offered him the five-pound note from her uniform pocket.

"Ay, maybe Song could drop by with some of those dumplins of 'is sometime," Derek said, passing her the change. "I'm not very good at cookin' for meself. It's been baked beans on toast for the past few days."

That explained the shop's fuggy smell, Max thought. "Sure, we'll let him know when we get home," he said. "Bye, Derek, and, er, welcome back."

The twins hurried out of the shop and into

the crisp evening. Kensy snatched up her bag and charged down the sidewalk. "Well, that was a surprise," she said, whipping off a glove to open the bag of candy. She shook the packet and picked out a green one. "I wonder why Derek was released. Do you think he made a deal to testify against the others? Or maybe he didn't know much about what was going on. He's not the sharpest tool in the shed, but he's got a kind heart."

"Song'll know," Max said as the pair pulled their coats around their necks and hurried along the chilly street toward 13 Ponsonby Terrace.

CHAPTER 4

FMXOV IFKVIG

Kensy burst into the entrance hall, where she was greeted by the wagging tails of Wellie and Mac, her grandmother's West Highland terriers. She threw her bag and coat on the parquet floor, then knelt down to give the two a pat and was rewarded with a lick on both cheeks.

Max closed the door and hung their coats on the brass hooks by the door. "We're home!" he called.

Footsteps thudded up the staircase from the kitchen and Fitz appeared, wearing his gym clothes and covered in a sheen of sweat. "Hiya, kids. How was school?" he panted, unfurling the black tape wrapped around his knuckles. "I heard about the fire."

"Ugh, not you too," Kensy grouched. She grabbed her bag and took off up the stairs, slamming her bedroom door when she reached the top.

Fitz turned to Max with raised eyebrows.

"Good news travels fast," Max said, ruffling Wellie's ears. "Who told you?"

"I had to call Magoo about something and he mentioned it. He also told me that Kensy's had a few hiccups lately. Were you planning to share any of this?"

Max grimaced. "Sorry, Fitz. I didn't want to tell, and a part of me was hoping it was just a passing phase, like the time when she decided to call all the teachers at our school in Banff by their first names. I am worried about her, though. It's as if she's pushing everyone away, me included, and she can't get it out of her head that someone's after us. You know she's like a dog with a bone when it comes to her theory du jour."

Kensy's bedroom door opened. "I heard that, Max!" the girl yelled, before slamming it again.

"Well, you shouldn't have been listening! We were talking *about* you, not *to* you," Max called up the stairs. He took a second to collect himself, then turned back to Fitz. "Any news from Mum and Dad?" he asked. There had only been three brief messages since Rome.

The man shook his head. "Not a word. I suspect they're planning to continue communicating via your watches for the time being. It's the safest way. Although I must say I had been enjoying your mother's cryptic notices in the newspaper."

Max nodded and hurried up the stairs, with Wellie and Mac following at his heels. He paused on the landing. "Do you really think Mum's parents are alive?" he asked, looking around at Fitz. "I mean, they've been gone so long. Could it actually be possible?"

After several months now with limited information as to their parents' whereabouts, Fitz had recently informed the twins that Anna and Ed were searching for Anna's parents, Hector and Marisol Clement. They were certain that the foul play the Clements had supposedly encountered in their Paris home had been staged. While their house and laboratory had been burned to the ground, with two bodies found inside, Anna and Ed now had evidence that confirmed they weren't the Clements.

"You know as well as I do that anything's possible," Fitz said. "Your parents and I were supposed to be dead too – and, obviously, we're not."

Kensy's door opened again. "Can you two speak up?" she yelled. "*Who's* dead?"

Fitz and Max grinned at one another, but before they could respond, the high-pitched whine of a performance-car engine coupled with the screech of brakes brought their conversation to an abrupt end. Max and Kensy ran to her bedroom window and were shocked to see their Uncle Rupert standing in the middle of the road, hunched over the hood of a silver Porsche. He was looking uncharacteristically disheveled, as if he'd literally been kicked out of the vehicle.

A woman was behind the wheel, revving the engine and screaming something incoherent.

"Whoa," Kensy sighed, her breath fogging the windowpane. She wondered which evil organization the woman worked for and did a quick scan of the rooftops opposite in case there might be a black-clad operative pointing a rocket launcher at him or some such thing. Kensy was surprised to feel a mixture of disappointment and relief to see that the coast was clear of any present danger.

Max unlatched the window and leaned out to get a better look. The wheels of the Porsche spun wildly, smoke billowing behind it. The woman released the hand brake and sped forward. Rupert, executing a textbook sideways roll, dove between two parked cars and escaped by a whisker. The car roared to the end of the street and turned left toward the city, the horn blaring in its wake. Rupert stood and dusted himself off. He smoothed his hair, straightened his tie and said hello to an old lady walking by with a puzzled expression on her face.

"Uncle Rupert!" Max called, waving wildly.

Kensy batted her brother's hand out of the way and shoved him aside. "Uncle Rupert!" she yelled, leaning out so far that Max had to grab her by the ankles to stop her from tipping into the street.

The man looked up and smiled. "Oh, hello, kids. Fancy seeing you here," he said, squinting at them. He jogged across the road and was met by Fitz on the sidewalk.

The twins ran down to meet their uncle. They hadn't seen him since his brief appearance in Rome. Kensy flung herself around his middle, hugging him tightly. "Are you all right?" she asked.

"Darling Kensington, I'm fine. Not a scratch, see?" Rupert said, amused by the girl's concern. He nodded at Fitz. "Good to see you, old man. I was hoping we'd catch up in Rome, but you disappeared into thin air."

"Yes, it was lucky we were both there, wasn't it?" Fitz said, his eyes narrowing.

Max didn't miss the look and wondered what it was about.

"Who was that in the car?" Kensington asked. "She could have killed you."

"She's not the first woman who's tried to see me off and I dare say she won't be the last," Rupert said with a grin. "She was supposed to drop me at the *Beacon*, but we had a little disagreement on the way back from lunch and I was ditched en route."

"That was your *girlfriend*?" Kensy asked. She wasn't sure if she was horrified or impressed.

Rupert shrugged. "I don't imagine so — not anymore, anyway. Now, who do I have to bribe around here to get a cup of tea? Where's that uptight butler of yours?"

"Song's out," Kensy said. "But I can make you one."

Max and Fitz looked at the girl in surprise. Never in their lives had they heard her utter anything remotely resembling that arrangement of words before.

"Consider yourself lucky, Rupert," Fitz said in a slightly wounded tone. "Kensy doesn't make tea for everyone."

Max scoffed. "Kensy doesn't make tea for *anyone*."

"Well, aren't I the favorite uncle then?" Rupert said with a smile. "Lead the way, Kensington."

The group filed into 13 Ponsonby Terrace and followed the aroma of a freshly baked chocolate cake to the kitchen downstairs. Kensy set about filling the kettle while Max cut everyone a slice of cake. To Fitz and Max's amazement, for the next twenty minutes Kensy barely drew a breath, gabbling on about her theory that someone was out to get them and going into great detail about what had happened when the twins helped capture the Brightside gang before they were properly admitted to Pharos. She even asked Rupert if he knew how Derek could possibly be out of prison already, but her uncle said he had no idea. Instead, it was Song who answered the question on his way down the stairs with the groceries.

"Ah, Miss Kensington, Derek pleaded that he had no idea what Esme Brightside and his mother and Ivy were up to and the judge surprisingly believed him. Then again, we know he is not exactly a genius, despite his tattoo that would proclaim otherwise," Song said as Wellie and Mac danced around his feet. "I hope you are enjoying the cake. It's one of Mrs. Thornthwaite's secret . . ." Song stopped on the bottom step and blinked in surprise. Wellie and Mac bundled into the man's legs. "Oh, good afternoon, sir. I didn't realize we were expecting you."

"We weren't," Kensy said. "It was a lovely surprise – well, lovely for us, but maybe not for Uncle Rupert since that awful woman kicked him out her car."

Max noticed Song shoot a look at Fitz and, again, wondered what was going on. Something about their uncle obviously set both men on edge. Song bustled over to the island countertop and began to unpack the groceries.

Rupert raised his teacup in the air. "Hello, old boy. Must be fun living in London town these days, away from the daily grind of Alexandria and all that polishing of silver and dusting of chandeliers – although I don't suppose it will last forever."

Song stopped what he was doing for a moment and removed his rimless glasses, before pinching the bridge of his nose. "Will we have the pleasure of your company tonight, sir?" he asked.

"You're off the hook this time," Rupert replied with a wink. "I've got a story to file before my date this evening, which, I must say, I hope goes better than lunch."

Kensy looked at the man as if he were mad. "Do you really think she'll be keen to see you for dinner?"

Rupert laughed. "Different girl, Kensington. Anyone who tries to run me down in a Porsche Boxter, of all things, is off my Christmas card list."

"Good to see you haven't changed," Fitz remarked from where he was leaning against the wall, his muscled arms crossed over his chest.

Smiling, Rupert sat back and folded his arms too. "You should get out there yourself, Fitz – have some fun and remember what it's like to be young again. You do still know how to have fun, don't you?"

Kensy giggled. "I don't think Fitz would dare," she said teasingly. "Not after Matisse Mayhew."

Fitz groaned and cradled his head in his hands. "Stop! Not another word!"

"Please, go on," Rupert said, his eyes twinkling. "This sounds like it will be a fascinating story."

"Mr. Fitz, I do believe you have been holding out on me," Song added, abandoning the groceries and leaning in.

"She was our neighbor in Thredbo," Kensy began gleefully. "And she was always dropping over to borrow this and that, and it was *so* obvious she was completely in love with Fitz."

Max nodded. "True. I mean, who comes to borrow a cup of sugar in a full face of makeup, a miniskirt and stilettos – especially when you live in a ski resort and it's close to freezing outside?"

"Well, you do know what they say – love thy neighbor and all that jazz," Rupert said.

"Did you take her out?"

Fitz scowled. "Only once, and it was under duress."

"They went to the fanciest place in town and, after a glass of champagne, she pulled out her calendar and asked what date would work best," Kensy said, stifling a laugh.

Rupert frowned. "Date?"

"For the wedding, of course!" Max howled. He and Kensy dissolved into fits of giggles. "She had it all planned."

Fitz sighed. "Right down to which font she wanted for the invitations. It was a train wreck."

"What a pity, sir. I am sure you would make a very handsome groom." Song turned to chortle at the cabbage.

"Yes, buck up, old boy – at least someone wanted to marry you," Rupert said. "And she doesn't sound that bad for a delusional psychopath." He stood up from the kitchen table and walked to the sink. "Lovely tea, Kensington, but I should make a move. You know, saving the world and all that."

"Already?" Kensy pouted.

"Sorry, sweetheart, but I'll see you again soon," Rupert said. He gave a wave, then bounded up the wooden staircase with Wellie and Mac hot on his heels.

"Traitors, both of you," Fitz said, shaking his head at the twins. He waited to hear the front door close. "Rupert won't be letting me live that one down in a hurry. He's always been a smug so-and-so when it comes to women. He used to do his best to make me and your father look like complete losers to any girls we were ever keen on."

"Sorry, Fitz," Max said, smiling from ear to ear. "We shouldn't have said anything. I can imagine Uncle Rupert giving you and Dad a hard time."

"That would be the understatement of the century," Fitz said.

"Uncle Rupert can't help it if he's a lot cooler than you and Dad," Kensy said. "Some people are just born that way." She blew on her knuckles and rubbed them against her shoulder.

Max rolled his eyes. "I know you think

he's amazing, Kens, but if you ask me, Uncle Rupert's tricky. He talks in riddles half the time and I don't think he ever says what he really means. And who has two girlfriends on the go at the same time? That's not very considerate to either woman."

"Considerate is certainly not a word I would ever use in the same breath as your uncle's name," Song said, running a colander of string beans under the tap.

Kensy bit her lip. Max had a point. Their uncle was a hard man to get a handle on, and she supposed that was why she found him so fascinating. One minute he was funny and helpful; the next he was making snide remarks and she had no idea whether he was being unkind or just stirring the pot for his own amusement. He was a liar too – she'd seen him tip his entire cup of tea down the sink. She shrugged. "I still like him."

"Confucius says he who acts with a constant view to his own advantage will be much murmured against," Song said, snapping the ends off the beans. "And, for as long as

I have known your uncle, I do not believe he has ever thought more highly of anyone than himself, except perhaps once and that ended in tragedy."

"Song!" Fitz barked.

The butler glanced up, chastened, then hurried away into the pantry.

Kensy and Max looked at each other. They'd never heard a harsh word spoken between the two men before and wondered what that was all about.

CHAPTER 5

DROGLM XIVHXVMG

Fitz turned the corner into Belgrave Mews and drove down the cobblestoned road.

"I love this street," Max said, admiring the pretty white Mews houses with their attic windows, wrought iron railings and coach lamps. "I can just imagine all the horses trotting along here, pulling their carriages."

"Indeed, Master Maxim," Song said. "Years ago these garage doors would have been wooden gates leading to courtyards with stables and servants' quarters above. Some of them are now separate houses, but most of Belgrave Mews

35

have remained part of the original mansions facing onto Wilton Crescent."

A single garage door opened on the left and Fitz maneuvered the car inside. Once it had closed again, the floor began to sink and they were quickly deposited beneath the London residence of Dame Cordelia Spencer and into a garage large enough to accommodate at least ten vehicles. The turntable spun around and Fitz steered the four-wheel drive into the space nearest the elevator.

The group hopped out of the car with Wellie and Mac in tow. The dogs didn't live with Cordelia full time as her city butler, Sidney, who also happened to be Song's twin brother, was allergic to them. However, the man could tolerate short visits once in a while, as long as they didn't get too close.

Song pressed the button for the elevator while the twins and the dogs bounded up the wooden stairs. The town house, set over seven floors, was vast and opulent like Alexandria, Dame Spencer's estate in North Yorkshire, just on a much smaller footprint. There was a beautiful rooftop garden as well as another large courtyard off the kitchen.

Wellie and Mac scurried along the hallway, their claws trip-tripping on the parquet floor. They jumped at the kitchen door, waiting for the children to catch up. Max pushed it open and was surprised to see his apron-clad grandmother standing at the stove, mid-battle, surrounded by an artillery of pots and pans. She enveloped the boy in her arms and kissed the top of his head.

"Hello, darlings," she said, reaching out to hug Kensy too.

"Something smells amazing," Kensy said, her stomach letting out a low rumble.

Cordelia wiped her hands on a dish towel and dispatched an empty pot into the wide porcelain sink at one end of the island. "I'm glad you're hungry as I think I might have cooked a bit more than we need. How does a lamb roast with baked vegetables, cauliflower au gratin, honeyed carrots, beans and peas and a frangipani pie with custard and ice cream for dessert sound? The pie is my dear friend

Faye's recipe, which I can't wait for you to try. Although I don't think I've ever baked one to the same standard as hers."

The country-style kitchen cabinetry was predominantly white, with a contrasting dark blue for the island. The room was certainly lived-in, with a pile of recipe books perched beside a crystal vase bursting with pink roses on the counter next to the fridge. A line of linen dish towels hung from the rail on the oven door. At the far end of the room, a small round dining table sat in front of a bay window with double doors leading to a terrace.

Wellie and Mac's noses twitched before they spotted their food bowls in the corner, each with two large bones fresh from the butcher.

"Oh, good, you've noticed your presents," Cordelia said as the two terriers scampered away to enjoy the treats.

The children sat down at the island and Kensy helped herself to a chocolate-chip cookie from a jar just as Fitz and Song arrived in the room.

Cordelia greeted Fitz with a hug and a kiss. "Hello, dear."

Fitz stepped back to appraise the scene. "You're looking very . . . domestic goddess."

"Good evening, Dame Spencer," Song said with a bow. He hesitated, frowning at the chaos in front of him. "May I enquire as to why Sidney is not in charge of the kitchen this evening? Perhaps we need to ask Mrs. Thornthwaite to come down to London to teach my brother some new dishes if his culinary skills are no longer to your satisfaction."

"Oooh, shots fired," Max whispered to Kensy, who grinned with chocolate in her teeth.

Cordelia chuckled. "You know cooking helps me wind down, Song. Don't worry, your brother is hard at work upstairs, putting away the crystal after the drinks party I hosted last night. Honestly, I didn't think Gabriel was ever going home. It reached a point where I had to ask Sidney to start switching off the lights."

"That's the prime minister she's talking about," Kensy whispered to Max.

The boy rolled his eyes. "Yes, Kens, I know – *everyone* knows that."

Kensy poked her tongue out at her brother. "I bet there aren't that many eleven-year-old kids who do."

"Well, they should," Max said. "It's called keeping up with current affairs."

"Very good, ma'am. I will go and see if Sidney needs my assistance." Song bowed and left the room.

Cordelia turned back to the twins. "So how was school?" she asked.

"Fine," Kensy said, a picture of nonchalance. She took another bite of her cookie.

Max shot Fitz a sideways glance. "Kensy set the science lab on fire today and we had to evacuate the building, but I'm guessing you already know that," he said, wincing at the kick to the shins swiftly delivered by his sister.

Cordelia smacked her lips together and deposited a vanilla bean into a saucepan of milk on the stove. "I had heard something."

"Geez, how many times do I have to say it? I didn't *mean* to," Kensy huffed, rolling her eyes.

"And you don't have to blab to everyone, Max. Besides, Vanden Boom said that there's no way that fire snake should have turned into a flamethrower."

Cordelia separated three egg yolks into a bowl and added an ounce of sugar along with two teaspoons of cornstarch. "I'm sure there's a perfectly rational explanation for it."

"Would you like a hand mixing that?" Max asked, hopping off his stool. He walked around to the other side of the counter to stand beside his grandmother.

Cordelia touched the side of the boy's cheek. "Your father was always helping me in the kitchen when he was a boy."

"Really? He hardly ever cooked for us. It was mostly Fitz or Mum. Dad occasionally tackled the barbecue, except he usually burned the sausages," Kensy said. "Mum makes fantastic crepes. Just wait until you taste them."

Cordelia locked eyes with her granddaughter. "And when do you think I'll have that pleasure?"

"Um, I don't know," Kensy said quickly.

"When they come back."

Fitz looked at Cordelia then at the children. "Your grandmother is aware of the situation."

Kensy and Max's eyes widened.

"Fitz briefed me, but we mustn't tell another soul," Cordelia said. "If I know your mother and father, they are more than capable of looking after themselves."

"Can you put more resources on the case to help them?" Kensy asked.

Cordelia sighed and shook her head. "We'll monitor things and, if your parents ask for help, I'll do whatever is in my power. Clearly, though, they have their reasons for going it alone at the moment."

Kensy thought that whatever was in her grandmother's power was probably quite a lot.

"I don't know how you've been able to bear being apart from Mum and Dad and Fitz for all these years, Granny," Max said. "It was easy for us – we didn't know anything about you. But if we had, we would have hated it."

"Oh, darling Max, it's been the hardest thing in my life," Cordelia said with a weary smile. "But just think what a reunion we'll have when your parents are back and we're all together."

Kensy nodded. "We should have a huge party, just like we did for Christmas except with better music."

"Excuse me, young lady, what was wrong with our playlist?" Cordelia peered at the girl over the top of her glasses.

"Nothing, if you like Elvis and country music," the girl said, grinning, as Song and Sidney walked through the door.

"Miss Kensington, how wonderful to hear that you have finally acquired some musical taste," Sidney said. The man muttered into his sleeve and a loud burst of "Now or Never" blared from invisible speakers.

"Stop! My ears are bleeding," Kensy complained, but Max hummed along with great enthusiasm to peals of laughter from the adults.

If anyone were to catch a glimpse of the scene, they would have thought the Spencers to be just about the most normal family on the street.

CHAPTER 6

ZM RWVZ

Saturday morning dawned gray and wet. Kensy lay under the covers, listening to the steady patter of rain against the window. She'd been awake for a while but, unlike every other morning in her short life, hadn't been able to face getting out of bed just yet. She was missing her mother terribly and her mind was still churning about the previous day's events. Despite what everyone said, she couldn't shake the thought that someone was out to get her and Max.

A shadow passed under the doorway.

"Is that you, Max?" Kensy asked.

When there was no answer, she reached for the pen on the bedside table that also doubled as a stun gun. The shadow moved and one of the floorboards on the landing groaned. Kensy sat up, her heart racing in her chest. She aimed the pen at the door, her thumb hovering over the trigger as she watched the handle turn and the door slowly push open.

Max's head appeared. "Whoa!" he said, raising his hands in surrender. "Steady on, Kens, that thing's a beast."

Kensy collapsed with relief and returned the pen to the bedside table. "Sorry, I was just being . . ."

"Paranoid?" Max glanced around the room at the piles of clothes, books, shoes, machine parts and other bits and pieces his sister had left lying on the floor. "To be honest, no one's ever going to murder you in your bed when presented with an obstacle course like this."

"Very funny." Kensy rolled her eyes and pushed back the covers. "At least I don't waste my time being obsessive-compulsive like you."

Max leaned back on the door frame and watched his sister wrangle her wild blonde tresses into a French braid. He spotted a soldering iron in a potted plant and shook his head. "Carlos is coming over later so we can finish our math research. We're going to the Natural History Museum afterward if you're interested. Apparently, there's a new exhibition."

Kensy groaned. "I forgot about that assignment. I suppose I should get started on it. The last thing I need is for Miss Ziegler to be on my case too."

"You're welcome to join us," Max said. It hadn't escaped his notice that Kensy was still in bed and that was most unlike her. She was always up before him and had been known to smash saucepan lids or blow a whistle in his ear to wake him up, which was especially evil given he was a light sleeper. He paused and added, gently, "Don't worry about what happened yesterday, Kens. I'm sure it was just an accident."

His sister folded her arms across her chest and raised an eyebrow at him. "That's a lie if ever I've heard one. I know you went back

46

to the science lab and took our ingredients to test them for yourself."

Max swallowed hard. He thought he'd done a great job getting everything without anyone noticing. "How did you know?"

"Ha!" Kensy leapt to her feet and began to bounce on the bed. "I didn't. Don't you remember that was a confessional tactic Mr. Reffell taught us last week? I'm so impressed it worked – and that means you're as worried as I am!"

Max's face fell. "Well, that's a big fat fail for me."

"What time's Carlos coming?" Kensy asked, still bouncing.

"Around midday."

She glanced at the clock on her bedside table and jumped to the floor. It was just past eight. "Perfect! We've still got time to test that theory of yours."

"*My* theory?" Max frowned. "I can't imagine Fitz and Song would be too thrilled if we set the house on fire, especially after what happened in class yesterday."

Kensy ran to the window and stared into the street. "I've got an idea," she said, spinning around to look at him. Her green eyes burned with mischief. "There's an empty town house right across the road. We could do the experiment in the cellar."

"No way!" Max exclaimed. "That's called breaking and entering, and if we get caught we'll be in heaps of trouble."

"Fine then, what do you propose?" Kensy demanded, folding her arms again. "Because if we don't test those substances, we won't know for sure if someone's trying to kill us until it's too late and, so far, since we've become part of Pharos, I can think of at least three occasions when someone has wanted us dead. We never got to the bottom of the crash with Esmerelda or the attempted kidnappings and, personally, I'd rather know for sure."

Max hated to admit it, but everything Kensy said was true and there wasn't really anywhere better to carry out their investigations. "Okay, fine. Why don't we pay Derek a visit after breakfast and ask him for the key?"

"Why?" Kensy protested. "I can pick the lock."

Max shook his head. "Not this time, and it's nonnegotiable if you want my help. You'd better get dressed and maybe at least think about tidying up. Otherwise you know Song will do it and he really shouldn't have to."

Kensy rolled her eyes even though she knew her brother was right.

Max headed down to the kitchen, where Song had just pulled a batch of chocolate brownies out of the oven. Fitz looked up and grinned.

"Good morning, Master Maxim," Song said, whipping off his oven mitts. He placed a bowl and spoon in front of the boy.

"Morning," Max said cheerily. He poured himself some muesli and filled the bowl with milk. The doorbell rang as he sat down.

All eyes flew to the monitor on the wall. Song peered at the screen before releasing the lock and admitting their guest. "Good morning, Mr. MacGregor," he said. "Please come in. Mr. Fitz won't be a moment."

"Why's Magoo here?" Max said, munching on his muesli.

Fitz took one last sip of his espresso and deposited his cup in the sink. "We're off to play with some new gadgets to see whether they're ready for inclusion in the school program," he said, folding up the paper. "Should be fun."

"At school?" Max asked.

"No, another secure facility in the city — I'll take you there one day," Fitz said with a wink. "See you in a few hours."

Meanwhile, Kensy was on her way down to the kitchen when she spotted their headmaster in the sitting room. He was standing by the coffee table, contemplating the painting of the stag on the wall. Kensy's stomach twisted. What else had she done lately to warrant a home visit? She was about to retreat to her room when the man turned around.

"Hello, Kensington," he said brightly.

"Hello, Mr. MacGregor," she replied, continuing down the staircase. "Are you here to see —"

"Fitz and I have some serious business to

attend to." The man nodded, rocking back on his heels. "And what are you and your brother up to on this delightfully dreary day?"

Kensy plastered a smile on her face, hoping *she* wasn't the serious business. "We'll be home studying. Math research assignment followed by a science project."

"Excellent." Magoo clapped his hands as Fitz appeared at the top of the kitchen stairs. "Right, we'd better be off. I don't know about you, Fitz, but testing days always make me feel like a seven-year-old boy at Christmas."

Testing days? Kensy wondered what the man was talking about.

Fitz gave her a wave and grabbed his coat from the hook by the front door. "Bye, Kens."

"Don't work too hard, Kensington," Magoo said as he followed the man outside. He turned back and smiled. "And stay out of trouble, won't you?"

CHAPTER 7

Z KVIULINZMXV

Kensy drew her raincoat around her ears and huddled underneath the umbrella as she and Max hurried around the corner to Mrs. Grigsby's newsagency. London looked as if someone had thrown a wash of gray paint over it, although it wasn't as cold as it had been.

"Seriously, I almost died when I saw Magoo in the sitting room," Kensy said. "I thought he was there to talk to Fitz about something else I've messed up."

"I wish we could've gone with them," Max said. "I'd love to be testing some new gadgets."

Kensy shot him a look. "Uh, I think we have enough to test for ourselves at the moment."

"Good point," Max conceded. He was carrying the ingredients in his small daypack as well as a lighter, a beaker, a set of measuring spoons, a bowl and a spare fire blanket filched from the pantry.

The twins left their umbrellas at the shop door and walked inside. The small television set behind the counter was blaring, but there was no sign of Derek.

"Hello?" Max called.

Derek's head popped up like a meerkat over the top of the shelves in the second aisle. "Oh, hiya, kids. I'm just restocking the tinned goods. We've 'ad a run on baked beans and tomato soup. Mostly from me," he said with a toothy smile. "What can I 'elp you wiv?"

"Do you remember when we visited Mrs. Brightside before Christmas?" Max started. "Before she went on her holiday. You came into the house while we were there."

Derek frowned and scratched his head through his beanie. "Yeah, I remember. Wish

I didn't, but that was ages ago."

"I think I might have lost my necklace in her house," Kensy piped up. "We haven't been able to ask anyone until now because you'd all gone away." She was counting on the fact that Derek wouldn't realize there had been a bit of time between them visiting Esme Brightside and the day the granny gang was rounded up by MI6.

"What's it got to do wiv me?" Derek walked around to the counter and dumped the empty box on top.

"We remembered that you were doing lots of jobs for Mrs. Brightside before she went on holiday and we thought you might have a key to the house," Max added.

"I'm not supposed to go there," Derek said gruffly. "It's off-limits."

Kensy wrinkled her nose. "Why?"

"It just is, that's all." Derek picked up another box from behind the counter and tore it open.

Tears spilled down the girl's cheeks. "Oh, Max, I can't believe it's lost forever," she said in a wobbly voice, and promptly burst into racking sobs. "I know it's only a silly necklace, but it was from . . . from . . . And now she's gone and my necklace is too."

Max hugged Kensy tight and patted her on the back. "There, there, it's okay. We still have our memories of her."

Derek stood by awkwardly, watching them. "Blimey, you're makin' me feel like rubbish," he mumbled, looking as though he might burst into tears as well.

"Have you got a key?" Max whispered over his sister's shoulder. "You don't have to come with us. We could pop down and take a quick look around then bring it straight back."

Derek's eyes lit up. "You're a genius, Max! You should get a tattoo, same as mine."

Max bit back a smile as Derek walked out into the room behind the shop.

"Ever thought about a career on the stage, Kens?" Max breathed.

His sister grinned. "You weren't too bad yourself."

Derek returned a minute later with a silver

key on a ring. "'Ere you go, kids. Just make sure that you bring it straight back," he said, dropping it into Max's outstretched hand.

The girl attempted a smile. "Thank you, Derek, you're an angel," she sighed, adding a final sniffle for effect.

Without a backward glance, the twins hurried out of the shop and into the rain, snatching up their umbrellas on the way.

CHAPTER 8

PZYLLN

Max crouched over the bowl and carefully measured the white powder before dropping it in. Unlike yesterday, Kensy was completely focused this morning, reading the instructions several times.

"Here we go," Max said, and clicked the lighter. "The moment of truth."

Being entirely encased in bricks, at least Esme Brightside's dank cellar wouldn't easily catch fire. He reached out and ignited the mixture, which began to burn far more fiercely than it should have. Still, it wasn't the explosive reaction that had occurred at school. He was just about to douse the flames when Kensy intervened.

"No, not yet. I tried to put it out with water, remember, and that's when it exploded." She unscrewed the lid of the bottle and poured a few drops on the burning mass. A bright flash illuminated the room and a jet of flame soared toward the ceiling. Max smothered it with the fire blanket and within a few seconds all that remained was a smoky residue. "I think that settles it," Kensy said, dusting her hands. "The white powder is definitely not baking soda."

Max nodded. "Judging by the way it reacted with the water, my guess is it's magnesium. We'll have to talk to Mrs. Vanden Boom first thing Monday morning."

"Do you believe me now?" Kensy asked. "It's obvious someone is trying to kill us – or at least me – and I think it's about time we find out who it is before they succeed."

Max began to pack everything away while his sister stood by and watched. "Could you give me a hand?"

"What?" Kensy replied, apparently lost in her thoughts.

"Never mind." Max shoved the rest of the gear into his backpack and slung it over his shoulder. "Let's get out of here. This place gives me the creeps."

The twins ran up the rickety cellar stairs, back down the hallway with its ghastly floral carpet and peeling wallpaper. Kensy opened the front door and peered out. The rain had stopped for now and the street appeared empty save for a noisy car sputtering past. She looked again and was pretty sure it was Derek's old green banger with the whale tail and giant silver rims.

"Come on," she said, dashing into the street. "I think that was Derek in the car, so maybe we should take the key back later."

"What if we –"

KABOOM!

Directly across the road, 13 Ponsonby Terrace exploded into a fireball. The twins were blown backward against Mrs. Brightside's door while a huge lump of concrete smashed through the windshield of a car parked at the curb. Debris rained down on the street. Max felt something hit him on the forehead. He sat against the door, dazed and confused. Kensy staggered to her feet. For at least thirty seconds she couldn't speak. Then the realization hit her like a bolt of lightning.

"Song!" she screamed. "Song and the dogs are in there!" Remembering her brother, she turned and gasped at the sight of him. Max was covered in dirt and blood, like something out of a horror movie.

He tried to stand, but each time his legs gave way beneath him and he slumped back against the door. As the plume of dust began to clear and people came running out of their houses, there was a cacophony of shouts and screams. Children were crying and adults were calling to one another. Someone yelled that they had phoned the fire brigade while another fellow shouted for people to get away from the building in case it collapsed.

"Max?" Kensy grabbed hold of her brother's shoulders and shook him. He looked at her, his blue eyes vacant. Her face crumpled and tears tracked two shaky lines down her dust-covered cheeks. Kensy glanced back toward the house. The entire front facade had been reduced to piles of rubble on the street.

A woman she vaguely recognized put her hand on Kensy's shoulder. "Are you all right, dear?" she asked.

"Song's inside. Please look after my brother." Kensy pressed the heel of her hand against her pounding head, then ran toward the house. Heavy raindrops spattered against her face. The front steps were gone and she could see snatches of flames in what was left of the living room. Kensy looked at a way to get across the missing landing and was just about to jump when she was pulled backward. She turned and couldn't believe her eyes. "Song!" Kensy sobbed. "I thought you were . . . I thought you were . . ."

"I know," Song said, enveloping the girl in his arms. She was trembling uncontrollably and struggling to breathe. "Miss Kensington, please, we must go," he said as two fire trucks roared into the street.

In a blur, Song guided her down the road and into a black taxi. Max was already in the back, as were Wellie and Mac. They scuttled toward her, whimpering, and she scooped them up in her arms, thinking she would never let them go. Kensy blinked and blinked again, trying to stop the world from spinning. She stared out the window and watched as the firemen connected their hoses and began dousing the flames. It looked like a war zone.

Song hopped in and gave the cabbie a nod.

"Don't worry, sir, I'll have you there in a jiffy," the driver said, pulling away from the curb.

Kensy reached over and clasped Max's hand, giving it a squeeze.

The black cab wound its way through the backstreets of London at frightening speed, then swung into a modest-looking mechanics workshop before a second garage door opened and the car stopped on a metal platform. Moments later, the vehicle descended into a parking garage. When they reached the bottom, a woman in a white jacket rushed out through a set of double doors. She was followed by two men pushing a hospital gurney. Kensy recognized her from their Christmas celebrations at Alexandria. All of the staff and families of Pharos employees had been present at the party and it was only then that the twins had realized just how many people worked for the organization.

"Doctor Foster," Song said, hopping out of the car.

"Hello, Song," the doctor said with a grim smile. "Let's see what we're dealing with."

The two men had Max on the gurney before Kensy unbuckled her seat belt. She took a deep breath and swallowed her fear. It wouldn't do her brother an ounce of good if she betrayed her true feelings. Her mind was racing. The science experiment gone wrong was one thing, but this was a whole other level of treachery.

CHAPTER 9

Z NRHHRLM

Cordelia Spencer stared through the glass panel into the room where Max was now sleeping. The doctor had removed a large shard of glass from the boy's hairline and had stitched him up with the precision of a master tailor, after which she applied a layer of synthetic skin, rendering the wound invisible.

Kensy wasn't at all surprised when Dr. Foster had pulled out the same device Mrs. Vanden Boom had used to check them over after their car crash at Alexandria. The RUOK 2.0 was a small tubular gadget that acted something akin to an X-ray machine and CT scanner, with a whole host of other features too. A hologram of the patient was projected in midair, displaying their vital signs. Apart from Max's cut and some bruises, the children had gotten away with barely a scrape, which was something of a miracle given the extensive damage to the house.

Kensy had been lying across three chairs in the waiting room after Song had insisted she drink a cup of tea and eat a honey sandwich. She sat up as Fitz strode into the room and whispered in Cordelia's ear.

"Scotland Yard is heading up the investigation," he reported. "They took it out of the hands of the Metropolitan Police as soon as you were revealed as the owner of the house. They'll be worried there's a nutter out there with a grudge against the newspaper."

"And have we got someone on the inside?" Cordelia asked.

"PA R2731 is in charge. Gas leak is the official line. She'll contain it so we can get our people on the ground."

"And what's the real story?" Kensy piped up, leaning forward in her chair. "It was a bomb, wasn't it? Max and I were meant to be at home. Song and Fitz were too."

"Thank goodness you weren't." Cordelia turned to her granddaughter. She'd barely been able to breathe when word had come through that there had been an explosion at Ponsonby Terrace. It was miraculous that Song had taken the dogs for a walk when he did, not long after the children had gone to the corner shop, and that Fitz had been out with Magoo.

"Now do you believe that someone is trying to kill us?" Kensy said. Her eyes widened as she remembered what they had been doing shortly before the explosion. "And we know for sure that the ingredients for the science experiment yesterday had been tampered with."

Fitz frowned at her. "How can you be certain?"

Kensy recounted what they had been up to across the road, in the depths of Mrs. Brightside's basement. "It was too risky to perform the experiment at home in case we set the house on fire," she explained, "which is ironic, isn't it, given what happened?"

Cordelia smoothed her navy skirt and took a deep breath. "Well, that's that then."

"What's what?" Fitz asked.

"I need you and Song and the children on a mission in Sydney, leaving as soon as Max is given the all clear to travel," Cordelia said.

Fitz eyed the woman warily. "Trainee agents aren't assigned to missions . . . unless the rules have changed overnight?"

"I've decided to break with protocol," Cordelia replied briskly. "As the head of Pharos, I can do whatever I want and the fact of the matter is I need two children watched like hawks. The best way to do it is to infiltrate the school they attend. Kensy and Max will befriend them and you can get yourself a job as a teacher – they'll only have been back from summer holidays for a few weeks and we can organize to have a staff member leave suddenly. Song can go too and look after you all."

Kensy's brow puckered. "Sydney . . . as in Sydney, Australia?"

"Yes, my hometown," Cordelia said with a sad smile. "I wish I could come with you. It would be a nice break from everything else."

"But the children have only just begun their training. Do you really think they're ready?" Fitz said. He had a feeling there was more to this mission than Cordelia was currently letting on.

Kensy's jaw dropped and she cast Fitz a dirty look. "Max and I took down –"

Cordelia held up a hand, stopping the girl mid-sentence. "The children proved themselves very capable in Rome and this won't be too arduous, I promise."

"It's your call," Fitz said, not missing the smug look on Kensy's face.

"Why do these kids need watching? Who are they?" Kensy asked.

Song returned with several mugs of tea on a tray. "Ma'am," he said, offering one to Cordelia.

"Thank you, Song." She took a sip and

straightened. "You'll be briefed in due course. I'll have some clothes sent from Alexandria and the rest will be taken care of."

Song frowned. Clearly, he'd missed something important.

"And you are to tell no one of your whereabouts – do you understand?" Cordelia said, looking directly at her granddaughter.

"What about Carlos and Autumn? They're going to ask questions," Kensy pointed out. "Our house just blew up."

"Fine," said Cordelia. "Your cover is that you were both injured in the explosion and you're in a secure hospital facility. After that you'll be recuperating at Alexandria until you're ready to go back to school. I agree that there is no way we can keep what happened a secret, given the damage, but we can control what comes next. Do we have a deal?"

"Deal." Kensy nodded, then slipped her hand into Cordelia's and stared through the glass at her brother. Her grandmother gave her a reassuring squeeze and kissed the top of her head. Kensy wasn't sure how she felt about returning to Australia. It was the last place she and her brother had been together with their parents before they went missing. But if Granny needed her and Max for a real mission, and it also meant they'd get away from whoever was trying to kill them, then so be it.

CHAPTER 10

HBWMVB

The electric gates opened slowly as Fitz turned into the driveway of a semidetached Victorian terrace in the suburb of McMahons Point, just north of the harbor.

Kensy peered between the two front seats. "Don't tell me," she said. "This is Granny's Sydney house in case she ever comes home for a holiday."

Song grinned and nodded his head. "You are absolutely correct, Miss Kensington."

"You're not a triplet, are you, Song?" Max asked. He was half expecting another of the man's brothers to be stationed here as a butler too.

"What a terrible thought, Master Maxim." Song squinted as he alighted from the vehicle. He had forgotten about the intensity of the Australian sun, which, after a drab and gray London, made everything look like a Mondrian painting. Song walked around to the trunk, fancying he would buy himself a new pair of sunglasses.

"So what's the story with the house?" Max asked. At street level, two arched windows stared out like unblinking eyes while, upstairs, French doors led onto a small balcony enclosed with iron lacework. The house attached on the right was a mirror image, though painted a lighter shade of gray. Down a short driveway was a single garage.

"It actually belonged to your great-grandparents," Fitz said. He took two suitcases from Song and led the way up the front path. "Your grandmother couldn't bear to part with it after their accident." Fitz pressed his thumb against a small pad above the door handle. It emitted a single beep, then opened to reveal a fantastically modern interior that looked nothing like the town house in Ponsonby Terrace or Dame Cordelia's home in Wilton Crescent.

Kensy and Max hurried in behind him, eager to get a look.

"Well, this is an improvement," Fitz remarked, setting down the bags. "The last time I came here, the place looked like it was stuck in the 1940s."

The interior of the town house was now situated firmly in the twenty-first century with a large, light-filled sitting and dining room at the front. Up a short set of open stairs toward the back of the house was a sleek, white kitchen with an island, a small round dining table and chairs, a laundry and powder room as well as a casual living area that led out onto a patio.

"There's a pool!" Kensy squealed.

Fitz chuckled. "I think that'd qualify as little more than a puddle, Kens. I'll take you somewhere you can swim laps tomorrow – just beyond the point, near Luna Park."

"Can we have a look around?" Max asked, but his sister had already bolted up another set of stairs.

"You can claim one of the rooms on the second floor," Fitz yelled after them.

That floor housed a substantial master bedroom with a bathroom and a walk-in closet and a balcony boasting harbor views. There were two other generous bedrooms with a Jack and Jill bathroom between them. Kensy called the slightly larger one at the rear. Max didn't mind, although the thought of sharing the interconnecting bathroom with Kensy didn't exactly thrill him. A third floor housed another enormous bedroom suite, while on the fourth floor there was a media room and an outdoor terrace with views of the Harbour Bridge, Luna Park and the Opera House.

"Look – there's a Ferris wheel," Kensy said, pointing out the window. She'd loved them ever since she was a little girl. "We *have* to go to Luna Park this time. Remember how Dad and Fitz said they'd take us that weekend we were in Sydney, but Mum wanted to go to the art gallery instead? Who knows how we ended up at the zoo."

Max winced at a sudden sharp jab in his head. He grabbed one of the outdoor chairs to steady himself.

"Are you okay?" Kensy asked, biting her lip. "Maybe you should sit down for a minute." She'd never been one to fuss over her brother, but she hated the thought of him in pain.

Max slowly lowered himself into the chair. "It's just a bit nasty every now and then. My cut must be getting better, though, because it's really itchy."

"You know, I've been thinking about what happened at the house," Kensy said, taking a seat across from him.

"Me too," Max said. He was glad that Kensy seemed to be acting a lot more like herself in the past couple of days and things were pretty much back to normal between them. In an odd way, the explosion could have been a blessing in disguise, although that was probably putting too positive a spin on it. "Fitz and I talked on the plane. He said it was a plastic explosive with a remote detonator and Forensics have traced its location to Granny's favorite Ming dynasty vase – the one Song fixed after the incident with that mysterious visitor when we first arrived in London."

"The bomb could have been in there for ages then," Kensy said. "I bet Song won't be able to put that vase back together this time."

"Well, that's where we're in luck. Song said that he'd only finished repairing the last of the cracks a week ago, so the explosives had to have been planted sometime after that or Song would have spotted them."

Kensy's eyes lit up. "That's great news! I mean, it's terrible, but … oh, you know what I mean. Anyway, who's been at the house in the past week?" she said excitedly. "We need to make a list."

"Remember how the washing machine was playing up and Song called the technician in to take a look, but he said he'd have to come back with a part?" Max said.

The girl smiled smugly. "Yes, but then I fixed it, so that was a total waste of money."

"And Mrs. Rodriguez had a cup of tea when she came to pick up Carlos after school on Monday night."

"Pfft, as if she had anything to do with it." Kensy stood up and walked over to lean against the railing. The harbor was busy with ferries and little boats and she could see a cruise ship heading in to dock at Circular Quay. "Uncle Rupert was there the day before it happened."

"That woman dumped him right outside our house. Bit of a coincidence, don't you think?" Max cradled his chin in his hands.

Kensy frowned and turned back to look at her brother. "Do you really think it could be him?"

"I don't want to," Max admitted, "but we have to remain impartial and consider the evidence, Kens. Remember what Mr. Reffell taught us about plots and suspects? Uncle Rupert was in the house in the week leading up to the explosion, so we're putting him on the list."

"But he helped us bring down the Diavolo in Rome," Kensy said. "I find it hard to believe that he'd help us one minute and want us dead the next."

Max sighed. "Think about it – he had time to plant the bomb. He was upstairs on his own on the way out."

"I hate this, Max," Kensy said.

"Let's talk to Fitz and Song," the boy suggested. "There might have been other people who visited the house in the days leading up to the explosion that we don't know about."

"I hope so," Kensy said, and the two of them made their way downstairs.

Fitz looked up from his laptop and was surprised to see two rather forlorn faces. "What do you think of the house?"

"It's great – it's also in one piece, so that's even better," Kensy said, half-heartedly laughing at her own joke. She plopped onto a chair and yawned.

"We've been thinking about who could've placed that bomb," Max said. Fitz closed his laptop and listened intently as the boy listed the names they'd gathered thus far.

"You should add my brother as a suspect," Song piped up from where he was jotting down a shopping list. "He came to deliver that batch of cupcakes you took for the school bake sale on Wednesday."

Kensy's jaw dropped. "You claimed that you'd made them yourself. Fibber!"

"I know, but I didn't have time," Song mumbled sheepishly.

"Were you able to retrieve footage from the cameras in the house?" Max asked, the thought suddenly dawning on him.

Fitz shook his head. "There's plenty of it, but nothing from the past week. Someone managed to delete it from the server."

"It was wiped? But how?" Max was incredulous.

"We have no idea," Fitz said, his mouth a grim line, "and that's what's even more concerning."

Kensy and Max looked at one another. Whoever had planted the bomb was likely a highly trained operative. So now everyone who worked for Pharos was a potential threat.

"Don't worry, no one knows we're here — not even your uncle — and your grandmother will ensure it stays that way," Fitz said. "She'll probably call in a little while. We have a secure line into the house, but if you do speak to her, do not mention anything about the mission. We never communicate that information over the telephone, in case someone is listening in."

Kensy walked over to the fridge and opened the door, peering at the mostly empty shelves. She pulled out a jar of stuffed olives and looked at the sell-by date.

Song collected the car keys and a handful of green bags. "I am going to make a quick trip to the supermarket. Are there any requests?"

"Violet Crumbles for me," Kensy said.

"Smith's crisps, please," Max added. "Just plain crinkle cut."

Song smiled. "I will pick up croissants as well. Confucius says that child with grumbling stomach will soon have grumbling lips."

"I doubt he did, but that's a good one, Song." Kensy took the olives and walked around to the other side of the island.

The man winked at her, grinning. "I won't be long," he said, and disappeared into the garage.

"Right," said Fitz. "I suggest you two take a break from your sleuthing and rest up for a couple of hours. We're due at school first thing tomorrow for your interview before you start classes and I start work."

"But I'm not tired and you've always told us the best way to get over jet lag is to spend time in the sun. Can't we go for a walk and have a look around?" Kensy asked, battling to unscrew the lid of the jar. She wrenched it open and fished about for an olive, which she popped into her mouth. Kensy immediately gagged at the taste and spat the offending item across the room. It pinged against the backsplash and landed on the floor. She jumped up, hoping no one had noticed, and threw the olive and the rest of the jar into the bin.

"All right, all right," Fitz relented. "I might join you for a quick trot around the block, then I do have a bit of reading to get through.

There are a lot of staff at the school and I want to nail my profiles so I can slot straight in – it will be much easier if I know the politics of the place. Why don't you two unpack and we can head out in a little while?"

"Sure." Max jumped up. "I definitely want to be organized before we start school."

Kensy rolled her eyes and groaned. Sometimes she wondered how they were even related let alone twins.

She and Max lugged their bags up the stairs and investigated their rooms. Kensy opened her suitcase and upended the contents on her bed while, next door, Max was painstakingly folding or hanging every item of clothing. As he took out his lint brush and set to work, his mind wandered to his parents. If his grandparents hadn't been killed in that botched robbery in Paris, where on earth were they and why hadn't they reappeared before now? It seemed crazy. Max's thoughts were running wild when, as if on cue, his watch began to vibrate. "Kensy!"

"What?" she yelled. "I'm busy."

"It's Mum and Dad," he shouted.

Kensy raced out of her room and down the hall, her green eyes on stalks. "What did they say?" She looked at her bare wrist and realized she hadn't seen her own watch since they'd left London, although she knew she had been wearing it on the morning of the explosion. Surely it was among all the stuff on her bed.

Max finished scribbling down the Morse code dashes and dots. "Getting close. Love you both. Mum and Dad." He looked over at his sister. "I wish we knew where they were. They're clearly getting closer to finding Mum's parents, but that could be anywhere in the world."

"Hopefully, it means they'll be home soon and we'll get to meet our other grandparents too," Kensy said. "Although who knows what kind of state they're going to be in if they've been held captive for the past twelve years."

"Kids, Song's back," Fitz called from the bottom of the stairs.

"Coming!" the twins chorused.

Kensy turned to her brother. "How much longer do you think they'll stay away?"

"As long as it takes," Max replied. "If there's one thing I've learned about this spy business, they're not working to a timetable."

CHAPTER 11

GSV XSZONVIH

Tinsley Chalmers waved to her children from the balcony as they headed down Warung Street, toward the ferry that would take them across the harbor to school. Her husband, Dash, leaned on the railing, sipping his coffee beside her. He was dressed for work in navy trousers and a crisp white shirt with silver cuff links, but was missing his customary jacket and tie. Dash Chalmers was a man who lived up to his name – both handsome and charming, he was much loved in social circles and generally considered the life of the party. In business, he was lauded as a generous boss who had maintained the integrity of his parents' company and continued their extraordinary work. Unlike his parents, though, Dash wasn't a pharmacist. From a young age, he'd been more interested in the business side of The Chalmers Corporation and had topped his class at Harvard Business School.

"Bye!" Ellery shouted, spinning in a circle so her dress fanned outward.

"Hey, Van, I'm looking forward to seeing that captain's badge on your blazer tonight," Dash called.

Donovan groaned. "Great, Dad. You've just jinxed me," he yelled.

The boy had had his hopes pinned on the position ever since he'd started at Wentworth Grammar at the age of eight. A total cricket tragic, he could endlessly spout statistics for various players and matches. Being captain of the first eleven was a huge honor and he knew that it would make his father incredibly proud to see his name etched onto the mahogany board in Darcy House alongside all the students who had gone before him – a couple of whom had played cricket for Australia. He sometimes wondered if his father wanted it even more than he did.

"Good luck, sweetheart," Tinsley trilled, waving. She turned and looked at her husband. "Hadn't you better get a move on too?"

Dash chuckled. "Anyone would think you didn't want me around, darling."

Tinsley smiled tightly. She poured herself a second cup of tea from the china pot and tried to ignore the sick feeling in her stomach.

"Lucy said my first meeting's been postponed, so I thought I'd have a coffee with my beautiful wife rather than sit in traffic," Dash said, gazing at Tinsley intently.

The moment was interrupted by Rosa, their housekeeper, asking if she could get anything else for them.

Tinsley shook her head. "No, thank you, and don't worry about clearing this. I'll do it. I know you wanted to make a start on the laundry."

"But that's Rosa's job, Tins," Dash scolded.

He winked at their housekeeper. "She's got everything under control. Haven't you, Rosa?"

The housekeeper nodded eagerly. "Of course, Mr. Chalmers, sir."

"Why don't you head into the city and get yourself something lovely to wear for the ball on Friday night?" Dash said. "Oh, and Lucy will watch the kids."

Tinsley sighed inwardly. "Dash, that's really not fair," she said. "The poor woman will have already done a full day's work and it surely falls outside her job description."

It wasn't that Tinsley didn't like Lucy – she was great with Van and Ellery and it must have been a challenge and then some, working for Dash. She knew he demanded a lot from his staff, and the fact that Lucy had stuck by him for ten years was something of a miracle. It's just that Tinsley sometimes resented how the woman was always about. And Lucy seemed to know more about her husband than she did.

"No arguments, darling," Dash said, giving her wrist a squeeze. "Lucy is happy to do it; you know how much she loves the kids and they adore her." He pulled out his wallet and peeled off an embarrassing number of hundred-dollar notes, which he threw onto the table.

Tinsley swallowed her discomfort and swept up the cash, slipping it into her pocket. She smiled at Rosa, who began to clear the children's dirty breakfast dishes. "Thank you," she said, feeling the heat rising to her cheeks.

"Well, I'm off. I'm sorry, darling, but I'll be late tonight," Dash said. "We're on the brink of a major breakthrough with the Influenza X vaccine and I need to speak to the press in the US. We can't delay the release any longer – the death toll in Asia has been horrendous."

"Mr. Chalmers, you are a saint," Rosa gushed. "The world is so much safer because of you."

Dash grinned and ran a hand through his dark hair. "Not me, Rosa. It's the clever scientists who do all the real work. I just make things happen," he replied, then kissed his wife on the forehead and walked inside.

Tinsley brushed away the tears that

had welled in the corners of her eyes and smoothed the imaginary creases from her pale-pink trousers.

"Mrs. Chalmers, you are the luckiest woman in the world to be married to such a good man who loves you so much," Rosa said. She shook her head, marveling at her own good fortune to be working for such an important family.

"Yes, the luckiest woman in the world," Tinsley repeated, glancing at the tiny camera above the door.

CHAPTER 12

ZMW HL RG YVTRMH

After the chill of London, Kensy was absolutely wilting. It wasn't just the heat that was confronting. The incessant chorus of cicadas coupled with the strong smell of eucalyptus was beginning to give her a headache, but maybe she was a bit jet-lagged too.

"I think we should head back home," Max suggested, eyeing his sister. He nodded at the copy of the *Beacon* tucked under Fitz's arm. "We could see if there are any more details about you know what."

Fitz grinned at the boy. "Your grandmother would be impressed to hear you say that. You know she's counting on you."

"And me," Kensy snapped.

"Of course, Kens – she's counting on both of you," Fitz said. He made a note to cajole her into having a rest this afternoon. It was a certain indication the girl was exhausted when she started biting people's heads off.

There was no sign of Song once they got home, although when Max walked past the video screen in the kitchen he noticed that the man was on the roof terrace doing a spot of tai chi.

Fitz handed Max the newspaper and headed upstairs. "Go nuts, kids. I've got to do some reading myself. I'll see you in a couple of hours."

"So, do you think this is a real mission or Granny's way of getting us out of London for a while?" Kensy asked, plonking herself down at the kitchen table.

Max shrugged. "Fitz said she was relying on us."

"I know, but don't you think it's all a bit too convenient that suddenly we're on a mission on the other side of the world?" Kensy ripped open the bag of Violet Crumbles and dived in. "Don't get me wrong, I'm not unhappy about being away from whoever wants us dead for a while; it's just weird missing school – well, *our* school."

Max sat down and spread the latest edition of the *Beacon* on the table. The front-page story was about the British prime minister cutting the ribbon on a new wing at one of the London hospitals. "We can't really question Granny's motives – she is the boss, after all. Anyway, these kids exist, and they must be in some kind of danger if they require surveillance."

"Go to the finance section," Kensy said through a mouthful of Violet Crumble. "I want to see if I can decode the messages the way Miss Ziegler taught us last week."

"I don't know if we'd be expected to work out anything that complicated. What about the death notices? They're easier, and

Miss Z said that was another favorite way to communicate." Max thumbed through the pages until he found what he was looking for. "Here they are." He ran his finger down the summary of names. "What about this? Grey, Sydney – that's got to be for us."

MRS. SYDNEY GREY
Departed this life 16 February. Much-loved mother and wife. Funeral plans to be announced soon. We take comfort that her suffering has ended and she is now at peace. Donations in lieu of flowers to Children in Need.

Kensy leaned in to study the text, scattering crumbs onto the page. She dusted them off, leaving a brown smear across the message. "Oops. How do we know which words we're supposed to be paying attention to, anyway?"

Max removed the page they were looking at, then turned to the daily cryptic crossword. He studied the numbers in the left column of the grid. "Look – write this down. Eleven, fifteen, sixteen, twenty-one, forty."

Kensy wrote the numbers, then Max counted off each word in the funeral notice until a phrase materialized: *Mother plans to take children.*

Kensy screwed up her nose. "That's not much to go on. Parents can take their children if they want to – unless she's intending to do them harm. I don't understand."

"Maybe there's a custody dispute and she's scheming to take them out of the country or something," Max said. "We'll have to check the paper again tomorrow." He smiled to himself. It felt pretty cool to be decoding a real-life message and not just one of the exercises in their spy classes.

Upstairs, Fitz was thinking that, so far, their mission brief had been exactly that – brief. Before their departure from London, he'd received an encrypted file with some pertinent details, including the names of the children Kensy and Max were assigned to befriend. A relatively easy internet search had revealed their targets to be the grandchildren of Cordelia's best friend, Faye Chalmers. The rest of the notes he had were about the school. They still had to find out the reason for the surveillance. Given the fact that Faye's son, Dash Chalmers, ran the world's largest pharmaceutical company, there was a strong possibility of a kidnap plot. Fitz was planning to update the children later that day and hoped they would discover more in the paper too.

He leaned back against the pillows. The last time he'd taken up a role in a school, he'd found himself teaching science. Thankfully, PE was more up his alley. A thought crossed his mind, and he hopped off the bed and walked into the closet, where he pulled down a pair of trousers that were hanging at the end of the rack. As he did so, the wall slid back to reveal a thin cavity lined with a range of lethal weapons. Fitz selected a small-caliber handgun and checked that it was loaded, then placed it in the top drawer of the bedside table. Although Cordelia was confident no one knew the children's location, he couldn't afford to take risks, especially when the evidence pointed to the fact that Pharos had a mole in their midst.

* * *

"This is *so* itchy," Fitz complained. He rubbed under his nose and sneezed.

Kensy and Max looked up from their notes and did their best to stifle the giggles that were bubbling up inside them.

"It's going to be weird calling you Dad," Max said.

Song grappled with the double chin, pressing it in place until the adhesive took effect. He then picked up a makeup brush and a pot of stubble and began applying a five o'clock shadow to Fitz's jaw. "Once this is done, sir, it will be there until the end of the mission."

"It's so real," Kensy marveled, peering at the man as if he were a rare specimen. "I can't believe how different you look."

Fitz glanced into the portable mirror that was set up on the dining table, turning his head left and right. "Well, that's hideous," he said, tugging at the double chin and wobbly turkey neck Song had conjured for him, "but it's still not as bad as the time Romilly was transformed into a hunchbacked hair ball of a man who closely resembled a troll."

Song chortled. "Oh, I remember that – it was a Christmas-party challenge many moons ago – Mrs. Vanden Boom's disguise was outstanding. So, too, was Mr. Rupert's. No one had any idea until a second Dame Spencer appeared in the room and we had to work out who was who. I am ashamed to admit I got it wrong," the butler said, doing his best to keep a straight face.

"Oh, wow, are there photographs?" Kensy asked eagerly. "Can we see them?"

"I am afraid that is not possible. What happens in Alexandria stays in Alexandria," Song said as he wrestled something rather large from the case on the floor. It was also incredibly unwieldy, flopping about all over the place. "Now we must complete the effect." Kensy and Max began to giggle as the butler held up the flesh-colored blob and pressed it against Fitz's stomach, instantly transforming the man's toned abs into an impressive belly.

By now the twins were laughing uncontrollably. Tears streamed down Max's cheeks.

"So when are you due?" he gasped.

"Any day, I'd say!" Kensy snorted. "And by the size of that gut, it's probably another set of twins."

"You two are incorrigible," Fitz said, but soon began to laugh too, which only caused his belly to jiggle up and down and make some rather nasty belching noises. "The headmaster might have second thoughts about the job once he sees me. I don't look like I'm at peak fitness, do I?"

"Um, not exactly," Max said, grinning from ear to ear.

"Then I'll just have to woo everyone with my undeniable skills and, if that doesn't work, my research has turned up some interesting notes on my colleagues," Fitz said.

Kensy's jaw dropped. "And what would you do with that information?"

"Let's just say, if I can't charm them, I

could always resort to . . . more persuasive means," Fitz said, waggling his eyebrows.

Song tutted. "Hold still, Mr. Fitz."

Fitz apologized and shifted uncomfortably in his seat. "Now, kids, let's go over what we know so far," he said.

"I still think it's weird that Granny wants us to watch her best friend's grandchildren," Kensy said, scanning the notes again.

Max frowned. "Whatever this is, Kens, it's personal, and if Granny trusts us to take care of them, then I'd say that's a huge vote of confidence."

"Which is precisely the right attitude, Max," Fitz said. Although he was beginning to wonder if the whole affair was little more than a domestic dispute and probably Cordelia's way to get the children out of London for a while.

Kensy rolled her eyes. "Well, I hope they're nice — even if their mother's a psycho." She threw her notes on the table and turned her attention to Song's makeup kit. The butler was busy putting the finishing touches to Fitz's gut, blending the edges of the belly into the man's skin with a pot of something that looked like putty.

"We don't know that for sure yet," Max said. "There's got to be more to it. Their father heads up the largest pharmaceutical company in the world, so perhaps he's made some enemies over the years."

Kensy pulled out a jar and grimaced at the contents. "He probably has," she said, unscrewing the lid and peering inside, "but there's been no mention of anything like that so far. It's the mother who's the problem."

"Imagine if your grandparents invented the domestic use for acetaminophen – that's pretty amazing, huh?" Max said.

Kensy grinned. "*Our* grandmother runs the most important spy organization in the world, so I'd say we're still one up on them."

"That is true, Miss Kensington," Song said. Satisfied with the appearance of Fitz's new belly, he began to pack up.

Max turned to the second page of notes

while Kensy pressed a fake wart onto her brother's forearm and giggled.

"Eww, what's that?" Max flicked at the appendage, but it didn't budge.

Song glanced over and shook his head. "Miss Kensington, those warts are just about impossible to remove."

"What!" Max exclaimed. "There has to be a way. I'm not going to school with a wart on my arm. No one will want to be friends with Wart Boy."

"Leave it to me, Master Maxim," Song said, and hunted about in the kit for something that might do the trick.

"Kensy," Fitz chided, shooting her a reproachful look.

"Sorry," she mumbled.

Song cleared his throat and made a face at Fitz. "Perhaps, sir, this is a good time to tell the children about . . ."

Fitz gave a small nod. He supposed he had put it off long enough, knowing the inevitable meltdown that would ensue. The twins looked at him expectantly. "Max," he said, taking a deep breath, "you're going into Year Six and, Kensy, you have to remain in Year Five."

"What!" Kensy spat. "Why? And we're twins, so that's just silly."

Max winced. He decided it would be safer to keep quiet.

"Actually, you won't be twins on this mission," Fitz said. "You're siblings born fifteen months apart."

"But *I'm* older by thirty minutes!" Kensy thundered. "Why do I have to be younger than Max?"

"I'm afraid it's not negotiable. It's going to be much easier to befriend your targets if you have things in common and the most obvious one is gender," Fitz explained. "I can roll out a whole lot of statistics to support the decision if you need me to."

"Don't bother," Kensy griped, slamming the jar of warts back into the makeup kit.

"Aha!" Song held up a vial of brown liquid that Max hoped was the answer to his wart problem. "Look on the bright side, Miss Kensington," the butler said. "At least the schoolwork should not trouble you, which will allow you to concentrate on the most important reason we are here."

Kensy scowled. She knew that was probably true, but it didn't mean she had to like it.

CHAPTER 13

SVXGLI ZMW NZIRHLO

Hector Clement leaned back and rubbed his aching neck.

His wife looked up from the other side of the laboratory. "Are you all right, *mon chéri*?"

"I am fine," he said with a weary smile. "And what would be the point in complaining? At least we are still alive."

Marisol emptied the pipette into the test tube and pulled off her latex gloves. "Perhaps we can finish up for the day," she said brightly. It was just after five o'clock and she was tired. The past few weeks had been all the more exhausting thanks to the sudden move. Marisol looked toward the one-way mirror and gave a nod. She had no idea if there was anyone on the other side, but acknowledging her departure had become a habit of sorts, and these days she was resigned to the steady drumbeat of a daily routine.

Hector turned off the Bunsen burner in front of him and walked to his wife, slipping his hand into hers. "We are getting too old for this. Surely there will come a time when they let us return home."

Marisol squeezed his hand. "I imagine, while there are billions of dollars at stake, nothing will change. Besides, I am almost certain that our home no longer exists." She pressed the buzzer. A loud click sounded and the door opened. They were free to go – to their apartment at the end of the passage. Wherever they were this time, it was a place of silence apart from the odd bleating of sheep or moaning of cattle. Marisol had begun to suspect a train line was nearby too. One night she had heard the faintest *clickety-clack* followed by a long whistle.

Almost twelve years earlier, Hector and Marisol Clement had finished their work for the day in the basement laboratory of their Parisian town house on the Rue des Barres in Le Marais. They had clocked off just after seven. Hector had prepared his famous coq au vin for dinner while Marisol had set the table in the dining room and opened a bottle of chilled champagne. It was to be a celebration because, after twenty years of research, they had finally done it. Their discovery would change the lives of millions of people.

Hector and Marisol had spent the previous weekend with their daughter, Anna, and her husband, Edward, when they had revealed their exciting news. Edward had promised that he would not publish a word in the newspaper that he ran alongside his mother and brother. There would be no fanfare until everything was in place. Hector and Marisol wanted to find the best home for their vaccine. It was too important and, after all these years, they would not jeopardize their life's work for fame and money. It wasn't about that at all and never had been. Their daughter and son-in-law had shared their own thrilling announcement too – Anna was pregnant with twins. There had been so much to look forward to, especially as the previous few months had been a little unsettling with two attempted burglaries at their home. The police had investigated, reporting that it was just opportunists, but Edward and Anna had insisted they install extra security measures as a precaution. Thankfully, life had quickly settled back down.

The Clements had gone to bed after eleven that night, but at half past two their lives would change in ways they could never have imagined. Marisol was the first to wake, and it took her a minute to register the presence of the heavily armed men standing at the foot of the bed. She had gently shaken Hector, and the two of them had clutched one another tightly, fearful of what fate had in store for them. When the tallest of the men jabbed Hector in the arm with a powerful sedative, Marisol knew it was far more serious than a garden-variety robbery. It was about their work, of course, but it had never been about what they could cure – rather, what they could unleash. And for the past twelve years they had labored, producing some of the vilest diseases known to man. In turn, they had also created their cures and, somewhere out there in the world, someone completely unknown to them was likely becoming the richest human being on Earth.

CHAPTER 14

DVMGDLIGS TIZNNZI

"So, what's my name?" Fitz said.

"Dad," the twins chorused from the back seat of the Land Rover.

Fitz rolled his eyes. "What's my other name?"

"Gerald Grey, but everyone calls you Gerry," Kensy said, itching under the collar of her new school uniform.

Fitz nodded. "Good. Where's your mother?"

"She died," Max said. Neither he nor Kensy were particularly thrilled with that story line, but it was the easiest way to deflect questions if kids got curious.

"And why are we in Sydney?"

"To avoid being murdered in London," Kensy said, garnering a glare from her brother.

"Because you got a new job," Max said.

Fitz nodded at them again in the rearview mirror. "Right. Keep it brief. Don't go into detail and, if you have to, answer a question with another question. Most people would prefer to talk about themselves if given half a chance, and the fewer particulars you have to remember, the better."

Song turned into a tree-lined driveway and through an enormous set of sandstone gateposts. The elaborate cast-iron gates had a "W" woven into their pattern on the left and a "G" on the right.

"After looking at the website, I thought this place was going to be a bit posh, but this is next level," Max said.

In the past the twins had gone to whichever school was closest to where they were living. They were always public schools and often underfunded, understaffed and in need of work. Max peered out at the emerald-green playing fields with their bright-white markings. An ornate Victorian grandstand stood loftily on the side of a rugby field, where several teams of students in black-and-white PE clothes were running through a series of drills. There was a white picket fence further beyond and a second grandstand.

Song continued past several smaller sandstone buildings before they drove through yet another set of gates and pulled up outside what could only be described as a mansion. Glinting in the sunshine, the Georgian-style edifice was at first glance at least three stories high and constructed from the same buttery sandstone that seemed to be the material of choice on campus. Kensy eyed a line of immaculately dressed girls streaming out from a set of double doors and gliding across a flagstone courtyard. She suddenly wished she'd brushed her hair like Max had told her to.

"Is this the poshest school in Australia?" Kensy grumbled. "And why is everyone wearing a blazer when it's already so hot?"

"I told you it was compulsory," Max said.

He had read the school handbook from cover to cover the day before. Kensy had flipped open the first page, but had abandoned it two minutes later. Now she was regretting the fact she'd left her blazer lying on the end of her bed. It probably wasn't the best idea to get in trouble with the headmaster before she'd even started.

Fitz suppressed the grin that tugged at the corners of his mouth. He was happy for Kensy to learn the hard way. "I can tell you there are far posher schools in England. Your father and I both dodged a bullet growing up the way we did. Sons and nephews of newspaper barons usually attend institutions like Eton or Harrow. As lovely as they are, I'm rather fond of old Central London Free – there was something grounding about it."

"*Under*grounding, did you say?" Max sniggered at his own joke.

Kensy rolled her eyes. "Was Magoo one of your friends when you were kids?" She couldn't imagine Mr. MacGregor as a boy in shorts.

Fitz tilted his head, considering the question. "He was in our class, although I'm not sure your father and I thought of him as a friend back then. He was a bit of an odd bod. I suppose he's still a little strange now, but he used to get up to some seriously alarming things."

Song came to a stop at the flagpole drop-off area.

"Like what?" Max asked, unbuckling his seat belt.

"A story for another time," Fitz said with a grin.

The three of them hopped out and stood on the driveway.

"I guess this is it," Max said. "Mission Sydney Grey officially begins."

Kensy tightened her ponytail and retied her ribbon. She looked at Max and Fitz. "Come on then – let's do this," she said with a decisive nod.

CHAPTER 15

XOZHH XLMUFHRLM

Kensy and Max walked through the double doors into the reception area with Fitz behind them. A middle-aged woman with a blunt bob and pinched lips was sitting behind the desk. She had a string of pearls around her neck and matching earrings and didn't look up from her computer screen. Kensy couldn't help thinking how different she was to Mrs. Potts at Central London Free School with her hand-knitted sweaters and broad smile. This woman looked as if someone had slapped her with a wet fish and then asked her to cook it for their dinner.

"Hello," Fitz said. "We're here to see Mr. Thacker."

After what seemed an impossibly long time, the woman dragged her gaze from the screen. "And your name?"

"Oh, of course, Gerald Grey," he replied. "And this is Ken–"

"Mr. Thacker is running late. Take a seat and he'll be with you when he's ready," she said in a clipped voice.

Fitz peered at her name badge. "Thank you, Ms. Skidmark."

The woman's nostrils flared. "It's Skid*more*," she barked.

Kensy snorted and quickly turned away to hide her giggles, while Max stared at the floor and tried hard to think of something to keep the laughter at bay.

"Oh, I'm terribly sorry," Fitz said, before ushering the children to the chairs on the other side of the room.

"I can't believe you said that," Max hissed into Fitz's ear.

"Me either," the man replied, grimacing. "Might be time for glasses."

After forty minutes of waiting, Fitz walked back to the front desk, where he cleared his throat. "Excuse me," he said.

Ms. Skidmore sighed heavily. "Yes?" she said, not even trying to mask the disdain in her voice.

"Do you have any idea how much longer Mr. Thacker will be? You see, I think I have a class at ten and I'm sure the children should be in lessons."

"I have no idea," the woman said, her lips barely moving.

Kensy bristled. Ms. Skidmore clearly hated having to deal with people, which was pretty bad for a receptionist. So far, she hadn't looked anyone in the eye since they'd come in, exuding a complete disinterest and total lack of respect.

"Ms. Skidmore, I'm sure that the school values punctuality and I really don't want to start off on the wrong foot with my students and colleagues," Fitz said with what he hoped was a winning smile. "Have you worked here long?"

"Long enough," she said curtly.

He tapped his forefingers together for a few seconds, then gave up and walked back to the twins, catching a glimpse of his startling reflection in the mirror. No wonder the woman was immune to his charms.

It was another fifteen minutes before the door to the headmaster's office opened and a man wearing a natty pinstriped suit emerged. Kensy and Max both thought he looked younger than they'd expected, presuming this fellow was the headmaster. His brown hair was parted at the side and lacquered to an unnatural sheen. He was followed by a young girl with a long auburn braid and a smattering of freckles across her slightly upturned nose. A thickset man stood beside her. Mr. Thacker guided the pair toward the front doors. There was much merriment among the group, with the headmaster fist pumping the air and smiling like a manic clown. He even looked to be miming something at one point, which had the three of them in stitches. Kensy also noticed that, from the time the headmaster appeared, Ms. Skidmore's eyes never once left his face. The woman either really needed her job or she had a huge crush on the man.

"Well, it's been a pleasure doing business with you, Mr. Thacker," said the girl's father. "I'm sure Lucienne is going to enjoy her time at Wentworth very much."

Max thought that was a weird thing to say at a school interview.

Lucienne turned to her father. "Will I be able to buy a pony now, Daddy?" she asked.

The man smiled. "I don't think we'll have to stop at one, darling."

"First-world problems," Kensy whispered to her brother. "Seriously, could they hurry up? We need to get to class – we have people to surveil."

Max hushed her even though he was feeling much the same way.

It was another ten minutes before the girl and her father left. The children couldn't believe it when Mr. Thacker turned and walked straight back to his office without a sideways glance. Minutes later, the external door opened and a tall woman with a brown ponytail and wearing a vibrant red pantsuit entered the building. She was nursing a tower of folders, which she promptly deposited on the reception desk and hurried around to greet Fitz and the children. Unlike Ms. Skidmore, this lady wore a beaming smile.

"Hello," she said, extending a hand. "Mr. Grey, I presume? We're terribly sorry to have kept you. I understand Ms. Skidmore penciled someone in ahead of your appointment at the last minute. I trust she's been looking after you?"

Kensy snorted. "Yeah right! She didn't even offer us or Fi– I mean, Dad – a glass of water," she said tersely. Kensy cast a look at Ms. Skidmore, who seemed to have a faint grin playing on her taut lips.

"Goodness, I'm terribly sorry. Let's rectify that immediately, shall we?" The woman's beaming smile melted quicker than an ice cream on a summer's day as she turned to Ms.

Skidmore. "Divorah, would you mind bringing some tea for Mr. Grey and juice for the children and a plate of that lovely cake I've just seen the cafeteria deliver?"

You could have cut the air with a knife as Ms. Skidmore pushed her chair back noisily and stalked off without a word of reply.

"I'll check that the headmaster is ready to see you now," the woman said. "Oh, and I'm his assistant, Stella Black – that was terribly remiss of me not to introduce myself," she said with a smile and disappeared inside.

"Finally, someone who isn't related to Cruella de Vil," Kensy muttered.

* * *

Following their interview, Fitz decided Thaddeus Thacker had all the warmth and charm of a brown snake – he was certainly no Magoo when it came to being student-focused either. The man spent most of the time talking about his own achievements and, strangely, only seemed interested in finding out whether or not Kensy and Max could sing. Apparently, the Wentworth

Grammar Choristers had won the Sydney Choral Festival a record five times since he'd been headmaster and he was aiming for a sixth title that year.

Kensy and Max could both hold a tune, but neither of them was likely to have a career in music. Mr. Thacker had asked them to sing a few bars of "Do-re-mi" and was practically leaping out of his seat when they hit each note. His elation wasn't shared by the twins, particularly when the man outlined the rehearsal schedule in extraordinary detail.

"Okay, kids, I'll meet you back here after school," Fitz said.

Kensy and Max gave a wave and wondered where Miss Black had gone to. She had told them to wait on the steps for her to show them to their classrooms, but the bell had just rung and there were children spilling into the playground from all over the place. Kensy glanced around and spotted a boy sitting under a tree with an open notebook on his lap. He was scribbling furiously and every now and then would stop to look their way as one might consider a zoo exhibit.

"I wonder who he is," Kensy said.

Max followed her line of sight. The boy seemed to be studying something intently, and that something appeared to be them.

"Oh, that's Curtis Pepper. He's one of our Year Five students. Lovely boy," Miss Black said, materializing behind them. "I'll introduce you." She motioned for the lad to join them. Kensy had barely blinked and he was standing right there in front of her. "Curtis, this is Kensy and her brother, Max," said Miss Black. "Would you be able to take them to their classes after recess?"

The boy beamed as if he'd just won the lottery. "I'd be happy to, Miss Black," he said, nodding enthusiastically.

The woman gave the children a wave and headed back inside.

"Do you want to sit down?" Curtis asked. "Even though it's overcast, the UV rating is off the charts and I forgot my hat."

"Sure," Max said, wishing he'd thought to wear sunscreen.

The three of them walked over to the bench under the shady tree. Max noticed pockets of children dotted around and felt plenty of pairs of eyes on them, which, having been a newbie at many different schools before, was a familiar feeling.

"So, whose classes are you in?" Curtis asked. He placed his notebook on the bench and took out a ziplock bag of apple slices from his pocket.

"Mr. Percival's," Kensy replied. A smile tickled her lips at the sight of the words "TOP SECRET" emblazoned across the front of the boy's notebook. "What's he like?"

"Oh, he's awesome!" Curtis enthused, swinging his legs back and forth. "He draws the most amazing cartoons. I've got Mrs. Hogan – she's even more incredible. She sings and paints and tells the most fantastic stories. Ours is the top class in Year Five."

Kensy's eyes narrowed. "The top?"

"Uh-huh. The classes are graded and you're in the second one; it's like the B class," Curtis explained with a smile. "Maybe you'll get moved up if you do really well in the first exams. That's happened a few times with new kids. What class are you in, Max?"

Kensy's mind raced. How was it possible that she could be in the second class? That didn't make any sense at all.

"Mr. Hook's," Max replied. From beneath his blond hair, he was shooting his sister warning looks to keep calm.

"Then you must be supersmart," Curtis said, clearly impressed. "That's the top class in Year Six. It's my goal for next year." The boy nodded emphatically. "Mr. Hook's nickname is Right – as in Right Hook. We reckon he might have been in a few scuffles when he was younger. He's got some interesting scars and he's not a man you want to upset."

"But I'm just as smart as Max is," Kensy protested, unwilling to let it go. "And, if you must know, we're tw–"

"Twice as excited to be here," Max yelled, glaring at his sister over the top of Curtis's head.

"Oh!" The lad jumped at the sudden spike in volume. "Oh, that's good to know."

"Where do you live?" Max asked in an effort to change the direction of the conversation.

"McMahons Point," Curtis replied, chomping on an apple slice.

"Well, that's a coincidence. We do too," Max said. He kept one eye on his sister just in case he needed to put her in a headlock to shut her up.

Kensy was seething. She stared across the playground, her hands balled into tight fists, until it dawned on her that she'd probably been placed in the B class because of Ellery.

Curtis's face lit up at the prospect of a friend who lived nearby. "Which street?"

"Two Waiwera Street," Max said.

"No way!" Curtis gasped, almost choking on his snack. "I'm at number four, which means we're next-door neighbors!" The boy jiggled up and down in his seat. "No one's lived there for ages, but they did this huge renovation recently. There must be some crazy rooms in that place."

"What do you mean?" Max asked, his curiosity piqued.

"Some of the building materials were weird for a house. There were sheets and sheets of tungsten steel and all the windows are quadruple glazed, and there was this guy with a van full of hi-tech electronics who was on-site for months. I tried to get him to take me on a tour, but he was really cagey and said the site was off-limits – it probably didn't help that he caught me snooping in his van," Curtis said. His eyes widened. "You'll have to show me around. I've been dying to get inside!"

Max glanced at his sister, who this time met his gaze. Neither of them had noticed anything particularly strange about the house. He made a mental note to ask Fitz or Song when they got home. Perhaps there was more to 2 Waiwera than met the eye.

"And we can catch the ferry together," Curtis carried on excitedly. "It's the best way to get to school. There are a few of us who do. Van's one of them." He pointed at a boy across the playground who was surrounded by a group of kids.

"He looks like Mr. Popular," Max said, taking note of the boy's confident demeanor.

"Van just got named cricket captain at assembly this morning. That's kind of a big deal around here," Curtis said proudly.

"Did you call him Van?" Kensy asked, the name garnering her attention.

"Yep, it's short for Donovan. That's his sister, Ellery, over there." Curtis gestured to a flawless-looking girl with dark hair. She was sitting between two other girls who were just as pristine. "She's in my class and Van's in Mr. Hook's."

"Ellery's in your class? But I thought . . ." Kensy looked at her brother. How was she supposed to keep an eye on Ellery if they weren't even in the same class? She'd have to get Fitz to fix that straightaway.

"I can introduce you later," Curtis offered. "Would you like me to give you a tour of the neighborhood this afternoon? There are heaps of cool places and some shortcuts you might find useful. I can show you where Ellery and Van live too."

"That sounds great," Max said, and Kensy smiled her thanks.

The bell rang and Curtis stood up. "Come on, I'll take you to your classrooms."

Kensy turned and glanced back at Ellery, who was giggling with her posse of gal pals. Surely, she wasn't going to be too difficult to befriend.

CHAPTER 16

MVRTSYLISLLW DZGXS

"Can you bring the donuts down here before you eat them all?" Max asked his sister, who had just dashed back up to the kitchen to grab her third one.

"Mmm, okay," Kensy replied, wiping her fingers on her school shirt.

Her brother walked across the room to take a closer look at his handiwork. He'd scored three bull's-eyes to Kensy's one.

"Well done, Master Maxim," Song said. "The balance on that hunting knife is particularly tricky. I am very impressed."

Max grinned and pulled it out of the wall.

"So, what is your new headmaster like?" Song asked.

"He's a weirdo," Kensy declared, trotting down the steps. She tossed her brother the half-empty donut box.

"What exactly do you mean?" Song said.

"Well, you know how Magoo's eccentric, but he's also kind and funny?" Kensy said, licking her fingers one by one. "Mr. Thacker isn't kind or funny. He loves himself to death and only cares about his choir."

"Perhaps he will grow on you, Miss Kensington," Song said, a hint of a smile on his lips.

Kensy scoffed. "Yeah, like fungus."

Max was glad that Kensy's mood had improved since this morning. She'd found out the classes were graded differently for math and that she was in the top group with Ellery, which had taken the edge off her being in the B class for everything else. Still, Kensy was counting on Fitz to have her moved before the end of the week.

Kensy held the tip of the blade and lined up the target, releasing it just as the doorbell rang. *Shooft!* It flew through the air, landing with a *thwack* somewhat off course.

Song peered at the small security screen on the lounge wall. "There is a young man at the door," he said, and quickly pressed a button. A false partition descended from the ceiling, covering the wooden practice board.

"That'll be Curtis from next door. He's taking us on a tour of the area," Max said. "Is that okay?"

Song nodded. "Of course. I suspect he will be an excellent guide."

"Have you been spying on the neighbors already?" Max chuckled.

Song raised his eyebrows. "Really, Master Maxim, what do you take me for?"

Kensy ran to open the door. "Hi," she said, finding Curtis peering at the fingerprint door lock. He had changed out of his school clothes and was wearing khaki shorts and a matching shirt. Coupled with hiking boots and a small backpack, he looked as though he was about to lead them on a bush trek, not a quick trot around the neighborhood.

"This is seriously cool. I've come up to have a closer look at it every now and then, but I've never seen it in action. You'll have to give me a demonstration later," Curtis said, his words flying a million miles a minute. He stepped around her and darted into the entrance hall. "I can't believe I'm finally inside! I'm almost tempted to call off our expedition and stay here. Oh wow, that's such a cool painting!"

Kensy grinned. The boy's unbridled enthusiasm was endearing. She followed him and, in a heart-stopping moment, realized that the lampshade below the painting was sporting something that shouldn't have been there. Her last throw had been wilder than she'd thought. "Curtis, have you met Song yet? Max, hurry up!" she called, adding a note of desperation in her voice that she hoped her brother would detect.

Curtis turned and thrust his hand into Song's. "Pleasure to meet you, Song."

"Likewise, Master Curtis," the man replied with a grin.

Max dashed back in from the kitchen to see Kensy gesturing wildly to the knife handle that was poking out of the lampshade. "Hey, Curtis! Let's get going. I'm sure you've got heaps to show us," he said, gently coaxing the boy out the door.

"Oh, okay," Curtis said, encouraged by the lad's interest.

"What's our first stop?" Kensy asked, pulling the front door closed behind them.

"The ferry wharf – one of my favorite spots." The lad handed them each a photocopied map and suggested they keep it in their pockets until they were familiar with the peninsula. Kensy shot her brother a wry grin, but Max just nodded and said thank you.

They turned right and headed down Waiwera Street, then left into East Crescent. Curtis pointed out various houses and announced who lived in them. Suddenly, out of nowhere, he leapt behind a bush that was protruding from one of the front gardens into their path. He grabbed Kensy's arm and hauled her in beside him. Max, wondering what on earth was wrong, ducked in too.

"What's the matter?" Kensy hissed.

Curtis unzipped his backpack and pulled out a pair of binoculars, training them on the house diagonally across the road. He fished out a notebook and pen and handed them both to Max. "Quick, take this down," he said. He glanced at his watch, which looked like one a diver would wear. "Seventeen hundred hours. Suspect sighted outside premises. Wearing suit and tie. Retrieving large box from Mercedes trunk with the letters 'LVMH' printed on the side. Entered house via side door at seventeen-oh-three." Curtis turned to Max. "Did you get all that?"

Max shook his head. "Sorry, I think your pen's broken."

"Oh, right, I should have told you it has invisible ink." Curtis pressed the side of the cap, activating a blue light, and scribbled in the notebook. "Okay, we can go," Curtis said as he packed away his things.

Kensy and Max exchanged quizzical glances. "What was all that about?" Kensy asked.

"I can't tell you," Curtis replied seriously. "If I did, I'd have to kill you."

Kensy giggled, then stopped when she noticed Curtis frowning. Without another word, Curtis picked up his backpack and led the children down an alleyway to a flight of steps. The ferry wharf was just across the cul-de-sac below. They walked back the long way so he could show them the park on the peninsula at the end of Blues Point Road.

"Where did you live before here?" Curtis asked.

"Um, Thredbo," Kensy said, hoping that was going to be Max's answer too. There was no reason to say they'd been in England.

"Nice." Curtis nodded. "We went skiing there in July. But the snow wasn't that great. Was your dad a teacher in Jindabyne?"

"Yeah," Max said. He was mindful of Fitz's advice to keep it simple, but he felt rude offering the lad such short answers. He scratched around for something to ask in return. "How long have you lived here?"

"Oh, all my life," Curtis said. "Which isn't really that long – ha ha! And what about the house – did your dad buy it?"

Max shook his head. "We're just renting."

"That makes sense because we didn't see it come up for sale. Mum's pretty sure it's still owned by Dame Cordelia Spencer and she's in England. Her parents used to live next door a long time ago, but they got run over by a bus," Curtis prattled. "Can you believe that? What a horrible thing to happen. Mum says that Dame Spencer is mega rich and she owns a newspaper called the *Beacon*. Do you know her?"

Kensy and Max shook their heads.

"So you're renting it through an agent then?" Curtis asked.

The boy was relentless. He was just about the most curious person they'd ever met. Fortunately, as they walked back up the hill, a silver Jaguar four-wheel drive roared past. Curtis stopped and waved, but the boy in the front passenger seat turned his head and the girl in the back ignored him too. The woman driving smiled and raised her hand.

"That's Mrs. Chalmers. She's super nice," Curtis said as he resumed walking. "Van's such a dreamer – he never sees anyone when he's in the car."

But Kensy thought that was a lie. Van had been looking right at them and turned away the second Curtis waved.

"Where do they live?" Max asked.

"I'll show you," Curtis said, and turned right into Warung Street. They caught sight of the silver Jaguar disappearing into an underground garage. Curtis pointed at a palatial pink pile which sat high into the hill, surrounded by lush gardens and mature trees. There were several balconies at the front and huge picture windows facing the harbor.

"Wow, that place is huge," Kensy said.

"Yeah, it's one of the biggest houses around here, that's for sure." Curtis nodded. "At least that's what my mum says."

"So, are you friends with Van and Ellery?" Max asked.

"We see each other every day on the ferry," Curtis said with a shrug. "But we hang out with different people at school."

The children heard Ellery bellowing at the tops of her lungs from somewhere inside the property. "Mum! Curtis Pepper is spying on us again. You have to call his mother. He's such a snoop!" The last word echoed into the street.

Curtis's face fell. He stood as still and quiet as a statue.

Kensy touched his arm. "Come on, you haven't even shown us the way around to Luna Park yet."

The lad's face brightened ever so slightly. "Oh, okay. Are you sure you want to go? Because we don't have to if you'd rather not."

"Of course we do," Max said. "You've been an amazing tour guide so far."

"Well, there's this really cool garden on the way," Curtis said, smiling. "It was built by a lady called Wendy who was married to a famous artist. Before she started fixing it up, it was like a harborside jungle and now it's gorgeous."

Curtis set off with Max beside him while Kensy stared up at the Chalmers' house for a few moments longer. She could see Ellery looking back at her and gave a half-hearted wave. The way the girl had yelled just then had made Kensy feel sick to her stomach, but she had to somehow look past it for the mission. She and Max had to befriend those kids in order to get to their mum, who was supposedly about to spirit them off somewhere. Still, Kensy hated the way Ellery had embarrassed Curtis. So what if he'd done a couple of strange things this afternoon? He was kind and friendly. Kensy had been to enough schools around the world to know that not everyone was. Even if Curtis had an odd habit of closely monitoring his neighbors, she had a gut feeling that he was a good kid, and good kids weren't always easy to come by.

CHAPTER 17

OLMWLM XZOORMT

Max sat down at his desk and smiled to himself. The irony of his and Kensy's life and that of their new neighbor had not been lost on him. Curtis, the amateur spy, had to be one of the most interesting kids he'd met in a long time, which was kind of comforting, given their other friends were so far away. His mind wandered to London and the bombing and whether his grandmother had any leads yet. It seemed that whoever was responsible was hiding in plain sight, which was disturbing to say the least. Just thinking about it made him wince, although maybe that was the residual pain from the gash in his forehead.

Max opened his laptop and was about to start on a comprehension passage when a call came through. It was Carlos. He hesitated, remembering what Granny had said about not letting anyone know their whereabouts. Surely, he could *talk* to his friend. He just wouldn't mention a word about the mission or where they really were – the only thing was, lying wasn't Max's strongest suit.

He hit the button to accept the call and Carlos appeared on the screen looking as if he were in the middle of getting ready for school. His shirt was buttoned, but his tie was hanging loosely around his neck and it didn't look as if his dark curls had seen a brush yet. He peered into the camera.

"Dude! Are you okay?" Carlos asked. "Magoo said there'd been a gas leak at your house and you and Kensy were in the hospital. I went by yesterday to have a look and – WHOA – your place is a wreck!"

"Um, yeah," Max said. "We're getting

better. I had a piece of glass in my head and Kensy's got a few bruises, but we're fine."

"Which hospital are you in?" Carlos asked. "I'll come and see you."

Max shook his head. "We're not allowed visitors at the moment – Granny's orders. She wants us to rest."

Carlos craned his head, as if he were trying to see past Max. "That's a pretty nice hospital room."

Max kicked himself for not being more careful. "Um, sorry, I think I can hear one of the doctors coming. I'll talk to you soon."

Carlos frowned. "Sure . . . Hey, Max? Are you really okay?"

Max nodded and quickly closed the laptop.

Meanwhile, next door, Kensy had taken a call from Autumn.

"Your house is a mess!" the girl exclaimed. "It's all boarded up at the front. I can't believe it was a gas leak."

"Me either," Kensy said, concentrating hard

on not giving anything away, even though she was bursting to tell her everything.

Autumn eyed her friend warily. "But it wasn't a gas leak, was it?"

"Of course it was. What else could it have been?" Kensy said, trying to sound bright and upbeat.

"Seriously, Kensy, you'll have to improve your acting skills if you're going to get something past me," Autumn said. "In the short time I've known you, you've evaded a couple of kidnappers – thanks to me and Carlos – you've escaped from a nutter in a taxi, you've survived a high-speed crash in Esmerelda that no one has ever properly explained, you almost set the school on fire and on the weekend your house exploded. I might have only been in training for a few years, but if I were you, I'd think someone was trying to kill me."

"Clearly," Kensy said with a sigh.

"So which hospital are you in?" Autumn asked. "I hope there are guards on the door." Before Kensy could reply, Autumn peered more closely at the screen. "Are you wearing a uniform?"

Kensy shook her head far too quickly and tilted the screen so that only her head and neck were showing.

"Yes, you are! What's goi–" Autumn's eyes widened and she placed a hand over her heart. "Kensington Grey, I can promise you that I am not on Team Kill Kensy and Max, so you'd better tell me where you are and what's really going on."

"Granny said we weren't allowed to," Kensy said weakly.

"Well, by the light in the room, I can tell you're somewhere sunny," Autumn said. "And it's bucketing down in London, so it's pretty obvious you're not here."

"We're in Sydney," Kensy said.

Autumn's perfect eyebrows jumped up in surprise. "As in *Australia*?"

"It was Granny's idea," Kensy said. "Anyway, we're both fine. You wouldn't even know that Max had a great big chunk of glass in his forehead. It's healed up already and he won't have a scar."

Autumn's hand flew to her mouth. "Oh no – are you sure?" she gasped. "Poor Max. That must have been so scary."

"He's fine," Kensy said. "And I am too, thanks for asking."

"Sorry." Autumn grinned. "Why Australia? And when are you coming back?"

"I'm not sure. We're on a mission," Kensy said. Now she'd really spilled the beans. If her grandmother ever found out, she'd never be trusted again.

"Wow, that's *huge*!" Autumn said, sitting back in her seat. She looked like she'd had the wind knocked out of her. "I assumed you were there because Dame Spencer thinks someone is trying to kill you."

"Yes, that's one reason, but you can't say a thing to anyone – not even Carlos. Granny will kill me herself if she finds out that I've told you all this," Kensy said, her stomach turning at the thought.

"Okay, but call me if you need anything.

Carlos and I can do some homework about the house explosion too, if you'd like. I'd better get going. There's an early lesson with Vanden Boom. We're getting new Pharos-issue running shoes this morning," Autumn said, grinning at the screen. "Apparently, they have many uses apart from sports and every pair has been tailor-made so we don't look like a bunch of dorks in the same sneakers."

Kensy pouted. "That sounds brilliant. All I have to look forward to is choir practice first thing in the morning."

"Choir practice?" Autumn frowned. "You?"

"I know – it's not by choice, trust me," Kensy said, rolling her eyes.

Autumn laughed. "Good luck with that. I'll talk to you tomorrow and, don't worry, your secret is safe with me."

Kensy gave her friend a wave and closed her laptop just as Song's voice drifted up the stairs, calling the children to dinner. The twins ran down to the kitchen and sat at the table. Fitz was there, helping to serve.

"We found out where Van and Ellery live,"

Kensy said, snatching a green bean. "The mother sounds really lovely – at least Curtis said that she was – so why we're here to protect them is a total mystery."

"Looks can be deceiving, Kens," Fitz warned. He placed a ramekin of soy sauce and a jar of chili oil onto the table. "Remember the charming Sister Maria Regina?"

"How could I forget? I'm scarred for life." Kensy shuddered at the memory of the nun gouging at the side of her face and removing a very convincing latex mask.

Fitz went to place the first bowl of Song's famous dumplings in front of Max but misjudged the distance due to his big belly, and it almost toppled off the table. Max caught it just in time.

"Sorry, mate," Fitz said. He leaned over further to make sure he didn't miss with Kensy's. "Honestly, this gut has a life of its own." He patted his stomach and sat down.

Song brought the other two bowls over.

"How was your day, Fitz?" Max asked.

The man ran his hand over the top of

his bald head. "Exhausting. On top of all my regular classes, I've landed myself a role as assistant coach of the first eleven, and they have a match tomorrow afternoon and then some super-important game on the weekend. Heaven help me, I haven't played cricket since I was a teenager and I must admit that I haven't watched it much over the years either. I'm going to have to read up on the rules tonight."

"You'll be okay, Fitz – we all have to fake it till we make it this time," Kensy said, grinning.

Max picked up his chopsticks and was about to tuck into his first dumpling when he realized the top of the lighthouse ornament that sat on the kitchen counter had begun to glow and the light was spinning. "Um, what's that?"

Song hopped up and pressed the door at the bottom of the lighthouse. "Good evening, ma'am."

"Hello, Song," the woman said cheerfully. "I don't suppose I've caught you during dinner?"

"Hi, Granny!" Max and Kensy called in unison.

"Hello, darlings. I miss you," she said. "Are you feeling better, Max?"

"I'm fine, thank you," he replied. "There's a bit of a pain now and then but no scar."

Kensy was itching to ask her about their mission, but she decided to heed Fitz's instructions that any discussion about it was off-limits.

"The builders are starting at the house next week, so things will be shipshape in no time," Cordelia said. "With regards to the incident, we're following every possible line of enquiry. When I find out who was responsible, they are going to wish they'd never crossed paths with Cordelia Spencer. No one threatens my family and gets away with it."

"You sound fierce, Granny," Max said.

"Fierce doesn't even come close," the woman replied.

The twins both swallowed hard, having just given away far more to their friends than they'd meant to.

"Love the wardrobe in the main bedroom," Fitz said.

"I thought you might," Cordelia said, her voice softening.

Max arched an eyebrow at Kensy. He'd been meaning to ask about the building materials Curtis had mentioned earlier.

"I hear you're looking particularly handsome at the moment, Fitz," Cordelia said, a smile in her voice.

Kensy giggled. "Only if round and hairy is your cup of tea."

"His chin wobbles when he talks," Max said. "It's hypnotic."

"Why, thank you, Master Maxim," Song said, his eyes creasing into happy half-moons. "I am rather proud of my masterpiece."

"You can all stop right there," Fitz grumbled.

"Sorry, dear, we shouldn't tease," Cordelia said. "What's for dinner?"

"Dumplings," the twins chorused.

"Yum. You do know that Song's are the best? Well, it's been wonderful to hear your voices," Cordelia said. "Love you, darlings." And with that the glow faded and she was gone.

"She sounds chipper," Fitz said.

"Why couldn't she tell us about the mission?" Kensy asked. Her forehead puckered with concentration as she wrangled her first dumpling with her chopsticks. She grinned triumphantly, then promptly dropped it into the little dish of soy sauce with a splash. Kensy tried fishing it out with her chopsticks, creating an even bigger mess, before giving up and using her fingers. She popped the dumpling into her mouth then, to her brother's horror, wiped her fingers on the tablecloth.

"Years ago, your grandmother made the decision that any information pertinent to a Pharos operation would be transferred via coded messages in the *Beacon*. Obviously, they've become more hi-tech over the years – especially with the advancements in augmented reality – but telephone conversations remain prohibited," Fitz said. "I'm sure there will be more information soon."

"But why?" Max asked. "That line must be secure."

"There have been some breaches that

nearly destroyed the organization – I'll tell you about them one day, but for now we all have to abide by the rules," Fitz said.

Suddenly, Kensy didn't feel very hungry anymore. Not only had she given away their location to Autumn, she'd also shared that they were on a mission. At least she hadn't divulged any other details and she wouldn't either. She could only hope that there were no bugs in her computer – or she may have just led whoever was after them straight to Sydney.

CHAPTER 18

GSV UVIIB

"Come on, let's get a good spot," Curtis said as he hurried down the gangplank, dragging Kensy and Max along in his wake. The boy swung into a window seat with Kensy beside him. Van Chalmers was already sitting behind them and Max slid in next to him, having briefly introduced himself in class the day before. Ellery was across the aisle on her own.

"Oh no," Curtis groaned, slapping his palm against his forehead. He leaned forward and unzipped his backpack, feeling around for something inside.

Kensy wondered what the boy was going to whip out this time. "What's the matter?" she asked.

Curtis sat back. "I forgot to take my pill this morning and I haven't got any with me."

"What's it for?" Kensy asked, hoping it wasn't anything serious.

"Seasickness," Curtis replied.

Kensy snorted, unsure if the lad was having her on. "Why do you catch the ferry every day if you get seasick?"

"It beats getting a bus and a train, and I get to be with my friends," Curtis said.

Kensy glanced across at Ellery. She'd only spoken a few words to the girl yesterday, but Ellery had already made it patently clear that she wasn't Curtis's friend and Van didn't seem to be all that keen either.

"Oh, okay," Kensy said. She nudged the boy's arm. "You're not going to be sick on me, are you?"

Curtis shook his head. "There's hardly any swell today and I have some special bags, just in case."

"Don't believe a word he says," a voice piped up behind her.

Kensy spun around. "What did you say?"

"Never mind. I'm Van," the boy said with a winning smile.

"Kensy," she replied, feeling the heat rise to her cheeks.

"You know I'm her big brother," Max said, barely keeping a straight face. Kensy narrowed her eyes and shot him her best death stare. He knew he'd pay for that later, but it was fun being the older twin for a change.

"I saw you yesterday in the quadrangle," Van said.

Kensy squirmed in her seat. She wondered if the air-conditioning was on the fritz. "Oh, okay," she said, and hastily turned back to face the front. Kensy folded her arms and wriggled down in her seat.

"Sisters, huh?" Max remarked, shaking his head.

Van grinned.

"Wow," Curtis breathed. His blue eyes

were huge. "You know, he was staring at you the whole time on the wharf before."

"No, he wasn't," Kensy hissed. "*You* were the one staring at *him*, and you should really stop that."

Curtis wiggled his eyebrows. "What are you — a spy or something?"

"Seriously?" Kensy eyeballed the boy.

Max had been adding mental notes to his brief assessment of Donovan and Ellery Chalmers while they waited on the wharf. The boy was about average height with a lean physique. His light-brown hair was styled and held in place with some sort of product, so he clearly cared about his appearance. Ellery was pretty with a dimple in her left cheek. She had dark hair that fell over her shoulders in two braids, each tied at the end with a perfect white bow. They both had an air of confidence about them. He wondered where they got that from.

"Is it always so busy at school?" Max asked. "The homework is a killer."

"Get used to it," Van said. "Wentworth Grammar is renowned for being hard work. Where did you go before?"

Remembering to keep it vague, Max told the boy they'd recently moved from the country. Fortunately, Van didn't seem especially interested. "Our dad just got a job at the school teaching PE," Max added. He thought he'd better drop that in or else Van might think it weird when he worked it out.

"What sports do you play?" Max asked.

"Cricket in summer and rugby in winter, although Mum would prefer I played soccer. She says rugby is way too dangerous, but I'm a winger, so I usually manage to stay out of the really rough stuff."

"Is your mother a little overprotective?" Max asked.

Van sighed. "Aren't they all?"

Max shrugged and gave a small nod. That wasn't a subject he wanted to get into, but he did need to spend as much time with Van today as possible, given the latest message in the *Beacon* this morning revealed that Van and Ellery's mother was poised to make her move. He and Kensy had discovered it while poring over the death notices at breakfast. This time the deceased was the aptly named Spencer McMahon.

A horn blasted and everyone on board turned to look. The cruise ship that had docked yesterday was leaving the wharf. The ferry surged forward to get out of its path.

Max's eyes widened as the two vessels barely made it past one another. "Close call."

"Happens all the time," Van said as the ferry pulled into Circular Quay.

They stood up and queued to disembark, finding Kensy and Curtis waiting on the dock. Ellery walked past and Curtis said hello, but the girl ignored him again. Van, on the other hand, couldn't have been friendlier – to Kensy, at least. He and his sister walked off together, leaving Kensy, Max and Curtis behind. The threesome were swept along with the crowd to the promenade, where Curtis directed them to turn left.

"Van must really like you," Curtis said, once they were on their way.

Kensy rolled her eyes. "As if."

"You don't understand," Curtis said with earnest. "Every girl in Year Six and probably half of Year Five has a crush on him. He's the most popular boy in school and he's good at everything, and I mean *everything* – sports, academics, even singing – though he's not a soloist in the choir. Until now I've never noticed him show interest in a girl and, believe me, I notice a lot of things."

Max suppressed a smile. It reminded him of the time a boy in Jindabyne was infatuated with Kensy and never left her alone. In fact, he nearly drove her mad, so Max could only presume how thrilled Kensy would be if Van made her the object of his attention.

"Stop talking, Curtis, and hurry up. We've got choir practice in five minutes and I don't imagine Mr. Thacker takes kindly to tardiness," Kensy said, picking up the pace.

She could feel the perspiration dripping down her back and her armpits were wet too. It was lucky she'd started using deodorant recently or she would have been stinky as well as sweaty.

"You're right about that," Curtis said, breaking into a trot. "Thacker's been known to keep rehearsals going right through until recess and there was one time we didn't finish until lunch!"

CHAPTER 19

XSLRI KIZXGRXV

The children dropped their bags among a nest of others in a corner of the auditorium foyer.

"Hurry," Curtis panted. "We're late."

"Excuse me," said a girl with auburn hair, "is this where the choir practice is being held?" Max recognized her immediately as the girl who wanted to buy a pony. She was sporting a bewildered look on her face. "Mr. Thacker said someone would collect me from the office, but no one came."

"You're in the right place," Curtis said with a nod. "Follow me." He led the group through a set of double doors into a tiered theater. There must have been over a thousand seats.

"Wow, this is a bit different than the hall at home," Kensy remarked as they hurried downstairs and back up onto the stage, where the choir was assembling.

"Good morning, choristers," Mr. Thacker boomed, tapping his baton on the music stand to make sure he had everyone's attention. He glanced about the group, his eyes coming to rest on the new girl. "Ah, there you are, Lucienne. Miss Sparks was meant to meet you at the office and clearly forgot." He glowered at a skinny woman with a cropped hairdo who was busy sorting sheet music on the floor. "Thank heavens you're a resourceful lass. Please come and stand in the center right here in front of me."

Lucienne smiled and took her place.

Kensy and Max looked at each other with upturned palms. It felt like yesterday all over again with the man ignoring them completely. But Kensy refused to be snubbed for a second time. This was also a perfect opportunity to capture Ellery's attention as the girl had just moved into her position on the stage.

"Excuse me, sir," Kensy said loudly.

The entire hall quieted and all eyes turned to her. A ripple of frown lines formed on Thaddeus Thacker's brow. "Yes?"

"We're new too and have no idea where we're supposed to be," Kensy said, gesturing to the stand of choristers. "Unless you'd rather we didn't stay?"

There were some nervous titters from several of the children.

Mr. Thacker ran his hand through his hair, and Kensy twisted her lips to stop a smile when she noticed it got stuck halfway. The man must have used a bucket of product this morning. "Oh yes, I remember you. Kansas and Matt."

Kensy raised an eyebrow and laughed. "It's Kensy and Max. Our dad is the new PE teacher."

"Stop it," Max hissed. It would do their mission no favors to get expelled on their second day.

This time there was an audible gasp.

Mr. Thacker's eyes narrowed. "Yes, of course," he said. "Why don't you go and find someone friendly to stand next to?"

Kensy scurried up to take a spot beside Ellery. The girl shuffled over to make room and shot her a smile.

"That was brave," Ellery whispered.

"Or silly," Kensy replied with a shrug. "I was hoping he'd forget who we were and send us away."

"Oh no, if you're in the choir, you're in it for life," Ellery said. She flicked a long braid over her left shoulder. "He'll be thrilled to have some new blood. All of his superstars left for scholarships at our archrival, Stonehurst. Mr. Thacker and their choir mistress, Simone Stephenson, hate each other. It's like one year we win the competition and the next year they win – it's been happening forever. It's our turn, but not at the rate we're going – we're terrible. Although that fat kid started just last week –" Ellery pointed at a solid boy in the front row "– and he has an amazing voice. I hope you and your brother can sing."

"Not really," Kensy mumbled. She had a horrible feeling that becoming Ellery Chalmers' new best friend was going to be more of a challenge than she'd first thought.

Mr. Thacker stretched his arms above his head and leaned to the left and then to the right. He puffed out his chest and rolled his head on his shoulders.

Kensy frowned. "What on earth is he doing?"

"Wait until you see the full routine – you're in for a treat," Ellery sniggered.

The man put his hand above his head and drew himself up taller. "Children, I want you to grab that invisible string attached to the top of your head and lift yourselves up, taking deep breaths, letting in as much air into the diaphragm as you can. Now wiggle your heads from side to side."

Kensy glanced about, amazed that the entire auditorium was doing the man's bidding. They all looked ridiculous!

"Just do it," Max hissed through gritted teeth. He was standing behind the girl, between Van and Curtis, and nudged her with one foot.

"Now, relax, but not too much. We're going to warm up those vocal cords. Ready?" Mr. Thacker nodded at the pianist. "Begin!"

The exercise involved an endless amount of *he-he*s and *ha-ha*s before they moved on to *mo-mo*s with their lips forming a perfect "O." The children gabbled and garbled and rounded and spat, loosening their lips and tongues for what felt like an eternity. Once she got the hang of it, Kensy thought some of the exercises were actually quite good fun – although she wasn't about to admit that to anyone, especially Ellery.

The headmaster's arms danced in the air as if they had a life of their own until a final flourish from the pianist saw the man's hands cross over dramatically in front of his chest before he pulled them apart as if tightening a piece of rope. The singing stopped and a reverberating silence filled the auditorium.

Mr. Thacker nodded his head. "Well," he sighed, "that was . . . better." He took another deep breath.

Kensy had to bite her lip to stop from giggling. The man was clearly mad.

"I heard some fabulous notes down here in front of me. There are new stars in the sky, thank the heavens for that." The headmaster winked at Lucienne and the boy beside her. "Now, this morning we are learning something modern and fresh and no one else will be doing it because I commissioned it for *my* choir."

The manager, Harriet Sparks, passed out the sheet music. Max thought there seemed to be an awful lot of staff dedicated to this one group, given there was a pianist, conductor, manager and apparently a woman in charge of styling and wardrobe too, which he later learned was the charming Ms. Skidmore.

Thaddeus Thacker tapped his baton on the music stand. "Open your ears to the most delicious sounds – and let's pray that the strangled cats who seemed to be running rife through the place last week have taken up residence elsewhere."

There was a titter of giggles, which Mr. Thacker silenced with a glare. As the pianist began to play, Divorah Skidmore scurried into the room and whispered something in Mr. Thacker's ear.

"What!?" he shrieked, his face turning the color of puce. "They can't change the dates willy-nilly! We need the entire term to prepare!"

Ms. Skidmore gulped and whispered something else.

"I don't care if the Opera House Concert Hall has to undergo renovations, surely they can put it off for another couple of months!" Thaddeus's chest heaved with indignation. "Two weeks," he spluttered as Ms. Skidmore retreated from the room. "We can be ready in two weeks. We have some of the finest singers in the country." Thaddeus Thacker sucked in a breath so deep it must have almost reached his toes. "Children, I need you to listen very carefully. Instead of the usual competition time in May, we will be performing this stunning piece at the Opera House in a fortnight.

And rest assured the Wentworth Grammar Choristers will win, because, children, winning isn't everything – it's the *only* thing!"

A tremor ran through the choir. While everyone seemed to be sporting looks of alarm, Kensy was awash with relief. This meant they'd only have to rehearse for two weeks and then this whole horrid affair would be over – and she and Max might not even be here that long if they fulfilled their mission sooner.

Mr. Thacker looked around the room. "Miss Sparks, get a message to the teachers that I will need the choir until recess and perhaps even later. Mrs. Strump, please begin."

The entire auditorium groaned as the pianist's fingers danced on the keys. Kensy was surprised to find the tune was pretty catchy. They then moved on to the solos, beginning with Lucienne. As soon as the girl opened her mouth, it was as if an angel had begun to sing. How a child that small had a voice that big was anyone's guess. Every person in the room was mesmerized. They burst into applause once she'd finished. If Mr. Thacker's smile grew any wider, he would have swallowed the small boy at the end of the front row.

Next up was a lad called Dugald – the new boy Ellery had unkindly called fat. He cleared his throat and began. Max felt a shiver as his rich tones filled the air. The boy's voice was extraordinary. Anyone blindfolded would have sworn the notes were coming from a grown man. By the end of the piece, the rest of the children were cheering and stamping their feet.

Mr. Thacker's face couldn't have been any more smug. "Now, perhaps the rest of you might like to present me with something resembling a tune."

"He's up to something," Curtis murmured to Max as Mr. Thacker finally dismissed the children.

Max looked at the boy. "How do you mean?"

"I don't know exactly, but I've got a feeling – in my gut." Curtis thumped himself in the stomach to prove his point and then blanched, having hit himself much harder than he'd intended.

"Everyone has their secrets," Max said.

"What's yours?" Curtis asked.

"Me?" Max scrambled for an answer. "Oh no, I meant adults – they always have secrets."

Curtis raised his eyebrows and gave Max a knowing look. "Sure, Max, whatever you say. You know, if anyone is going to uncover the secrets around here, it's me. It's what I do. You'll see."

Max grinned. If only Curtis knew.

CHAPTER 20

RMGVIMZO XLMUORXG

After recess, the children had math, which meant Kensy could spend more time cozying up to Ellery. When their teacher announced a new project that required the students to work in pairs, Kensy made a beeline for the girl, much to Curtis's disappointment. She felt bad fobbing him off, but it couldn't be helped.

Meanwhile, in 6H, Max had managed to sit across from Van and snatch a couple of quick conversations during the lessons before lunch. He asked for the boy's help with a comprehension exercise and another activity he said he couldn't understand, gently stroking Van's sizable ego and wheedling his way into a friendship. As for their teacher, Max decided that Mr. Hook's reputation was far worse than the man deserved. Fair enough, he had a leery look which silenced the class in a nanosecond, but apart from that he never raised his voice. His teaching style was rather dull, especially compared to Mr. Reffell's nutty antics, and he would never have won an argument against Miss Witherbee.

As they were packing up their things, Max leaned forward and tapped Van on the shoulder. "What do we have this afternoon?" he asked.

"Do you need to get your glasses checked?" the lad said with a grin. He motioned toward the front of the room, where it was clearly written on the whiteboard that they had a year-group meeting followed by science.

"Oh, sorry, that was silly of me. Just finding my feet," Max said, feeling like an idiot. "Is there somewhere you usually sit at lunchtime? I mean, the Year Sixes?"

"You can hang out with me, if you like," Van said. "But I have to see Mr. De Vere about the cricket match on the weekend. We're playing on Bradman Oval in Bowral against a team from Moss Vale."

None of that meant a thing to Max and his face must have betrayed his lack of knowledge.

Van looked at the lad quizzically. "You do know who Sir Donald Bradman was, right?"

"Sure." Max nodded, hoping Van wouldn't ask him anything more. He'd be looking that up as soon as he got home. "My dad's the new assistant coach of your team," he said, as the pair retrieved their lunch boxes from the lockers and walked out to the courtyard. "What do your parents do?"

"Dad runs a company and Mum looks after us – when she's not shopping or having her hair done or going to lunch with friends," Van replied. "What about your mum?"

Max shook his head. "She's not around."

Fortunately, Van left it at that. Max couldn't work out of if the boy was sympathetic or if he didn't really care. Either was fine as Max preferred not to weave the web of lies any tighter than he needed to. The deceit was one of the things that bothered him most about his new career path. It wasn't something that came naturally at all; no wonder they had to have specialist lessons in the craft.

The playground seemed clearly marked by year-group boundaries. Max sat with Van and some of his friends on a patch of grass beneath a leafy oak tree while he spied Kensy with Curtis on the seats outside the entrance to the Year Five block. Ellery was nowhere in sight.

"So, what's your sister like?" Van asked out of the blue.

"Oh, Kensy?" Max faltered. "She's funny and blunt and she's really clever. Don't tell her I said so, but she's probably a better skier than me – technically, at least."

"It sounds as if you actually like her," Van said.

"Most of the time. We have our moments. Why? Don't you get along with your sister?"

Van shrugged. "She's okay in small doses, but she can be a total brat. She's really good at getting her own way with Dad. I wouldn't necessarily choose to hang out with her, but maybe she and Kensy will be friends."

Max spotted Ellery and a posse of three girls heading toward Kensy and Curtis. They stopped in front of them, blocking out the sun.

Kensy looked up. "Hi," she said. She knew that one of the girls was called Ruby, another was Mia and the third was Candice. Ruby was in her homeroom class, while the other two were in Mr. Percival's math class.

"Would you like to come and sit with us?" Ellery asked.

Kensy looked at Curtis, whose blue eyes instantly brightened.

"Sure, thanks," Kensy said. She and Curtis both stood up.

Ellery giggled. "Not you, Pepper. *As if.*"

The other three girls laughed.

Kensy's first instinct was to tell them that, if Curtis wasn't invited, she didn't care to be with them either. She had to fight her fury as her mouth opened before she clamped it shut again. Ellery was her mission. Curtis was her neighbor and for how long was anyone's guess. She had to rationalize it this way or else it hurt too much. Being a spy was much harder on her emotions than she'd thought it would be.

"Well, are you coming or not?" Ellery asked, flicking a braid over her shoulder.

Kensy hesitated, then picked up her lunch box. "I'll catch you after school," she whispered to Curtis.

"Oh." The boy quickly smiled and nodded. "Okay, see you on the ferry."

Kensy waved and walked off with the girls, hating herself more than she had for a very long time. In her head, she kept repeating that this was her job and she had no choice, but right at that moment, all she wanted was to rush back to Curtis and give him a great big hug.

CHAPTER 21

KOZMH

Tinsley Chalmers pulled the letter out of her handbag and opened it. She read the words again – confirmation that staying was no longer an option. There was no one she could tell – who would believe her? Her heart was pounding as she contemplated her next move. It would be the biggest of her life. All the way to France. She had already purchased the farmhouse in a little village just outside Bergerac in the Dordogne region. It was a place she had spent some time after university, before she'd met Dash and been swept off her feet. Strangely, it wasn't an adventure she'd ever told him about, even though she'd lived there as a nanny for six months. Bergerac was her escape route. She would take the children and, if things went according to plan, he would never find them – at least until they wanted to be found. The children would hate her to begin with. She was fully prepared for that.

While Tinsley hadn't earned a cent of her own money since Van and Ellery were born, for the past five years she'd had a nest egg locked away in a term deposit. It had come as a complete shock upon her father's death to learn that he had left her over six hundred thousand dollars. Unlike her husband's family, her own parents weren't wealthy, though they were fiercely proud, which was probably why Dash hadn't bothered to attend the reading of the will with her. Tinsley had been so enamored by her husband and his glamorous and exciting life. It galled her to think of the way she'd abandoned her family – that she'd felt embarrassed by them when they were the people who had truly loved her the most in the world. They were the best sort of people, but that was something she'd realized far too late.

Tinsley looked up the address of the travel agent. She needed to go to the bank first and withdraw the money. There was no way she could touch the joint account she shared with Dash – he questioned the tiniest amount, even the weekly grocery bill. Everything had to be paid in cash with no paper trail and they were certainly taking the long way around. Three tickets to New York. Then they would need false passports so they could leave their old life far behind. That part of the process was proving a little trickier. Tinsley didn't know any criminals, but this afternoon she was planning to meet one. She just had to be back in time to pick up Ellery from her dance class and Van from cricket and the clock was ticking.

CHAPTER 22

ZMW GSVIV SV TLVH ZTZRM

Kensy dumped her backpack on the seat beside her brother and sat down.

"How was your dance class?" Max asked, without taking his eyes off the field.

"It's not really my thing," she said. "But Ellery's into it and I think I've managed to convince her that I am too. She's asked us round for a swim when we get home. Have you worked out a way to get yourself on the team yet?"

Max turned to look at her. "You can't be serious. I've never played more than beach cricket. And that's the top team you're talking about – I'd be lucky to make the lower team here."

"Well, I hate to point out the obvious, but it'll be easier to stay close to Van if you're out there with him," the girl replied.

On the field, Van had just directed a couple more of the boys to stand in closer to the batsman.

"Come on, this one's ours," shouted a tall lad.

At the bowler's end, Van took his run-up, past Fitz, who was umpiring, and sent the ball flying down the pitch, smashing the middle stump clean out of the ground.

"Howzat!" Van shouted. He and his team-mates leapt into the air, having just claimed another St. Mark's wicket. Fitz raised his pointer finger in the air to give the batsman out.

"I've got an idea," Kensy said with a glint in her eye. She reached into her schoolbag and retrieved a tiny ring box.

"What? Oh no," Max said, shaking his head. "You said it wasn't ready yet."

Kensy shrugged. "Maybe it isn't, but this is the perfect place to test it out. Your poison-dart glasses haven't got a long enough range, so this is the next best thing. Don't be such a wuss."

Max watched as his sister pulled out what looked like a bee and a tiny controller. She'd been working on it for weeks now and, having most recently chased Song around the kitchen with it, was very pleased with her handiwork.

Kensy fished about for her glasses, which were in another case at the bottom of her bag. She put them on, then pressed the invisible button on the side. "Here goes nothing," she said as the insect whirred to life. She stood up and eyed her target – a skinny lad near the fence closest to them. Via the controller and her magnified glasses, she maneuvered the insect toward the boy, landing it on the back of his neck so gently he didn't feel a thing.

Van took his run-up for the last ball of the innings, but stopped short when the lad clutched his neck and began to scream. "Something stung me!" the boy yelped.

Another fielder ran over to help and was soon jumping around and shouting too. A third wound up squealing like a stuck pig. All the while, Kensy couldn't help giggling. Her bee was perfection and, while its victims might have felt a sharp pinprick, there was no venom in the sting. It was just a jab – at least until she could work out how to store a liquid sedative in it, but she was going to need a lot more help with that.

Fitz stopped play and the Wentworth head coach, Jaco De Vere, raced onto the field.

"Pfft, what a load of carrying-on for a fake bee sting," Kensy said, rolling her eyes. She held out her hand for the bee to land on and packed it away, popping the case, glasses and controller into her bag.

"Good job, *little* sister," Max said, grinning.

Kensy shot him a warning look. "Really? You really want to go there, after seeing what my bee can do?"

The skinny lad was now the color of his cricket whites. "Sir, I'm allergic to bees," he whimpered.

Jaco wasn't prepared to take any chances and was on the phone to the school nurse, who arrived at the ground minutes later. She whisked the three boys back to the infirmary, where she was going to keep them under observation until their parents arrived. Jaco called to Fitz, who was busy checking the score and hoping to goodness he hadn't made any mistakes. He walked to the bottom of the grandstand. "Gerry, we're going to be a player short. Is your boy perchance any good with a bat?"

Fitz was wondering if they might call off the rest of the game, but apparently cricket was more important than a few boys with bee stings and potentially life-threatening allergic reactions. Wentworth Grammar were due to go in to bat after a short water break.

"You can thank me later, *little* brother," Kensy said, nudging Max in the ribs.

"I'd love to play, except I don't have a uniform," Max yelled to the coach.

Mr. De Vere held up his hand. "Leave that to me." The man made another call and not twenty minutes later a young fellow arrived with a bag of cricket whites.

By the time Max emerged, ready for action, the home team was four wickets down. Van was batting and the only one to be scoring any runs. There was a shout and Fitz's finger rose into the air again. Five down. It seemed that St. Mark's was about to give Wentworth Grammar a lesson in how to play cricket.

"You're up, Max," Jaco De Vere said, to the boy's great surprise.

"But I thought it was Ted's turn . . ." Max frowned at a stocky lad with red hair who was scoffing a bag of crinkle-cut chips.

"I already know how he plays, but I haven't seen you in action," the coach said. "And we might be in need of some new blood for the weekend, if you're any good. I have a feeling Errol's mother will take him home and wrap him up in a big wad of cotton for a month. BJ's is just as likely to do the same."

Max had already padded and gloved up. He put on the helmet, then spent a couple of seconds trying to think if he had everything he needed.

Ted looked at him. "What about Hector?" he asked.

Max frowned. He couldn't remember any of the boys being called Hector.

The boy tapped his crotch, which echoed loudly. "Hector the protector. You don't want a googly in the gonads." The boy made a face. "Trust me."

Max quickly grabbed the thing and stuffed it into his trousers, hoping that no one was watching. Then he picked up a bat and trotted down the stairs and onto the oval.

"Go, Max!" Ted shouted, giving the boy in front of him a chip shower.

"Show them how it's done, Max," Kensy called.

At the crease, Van glanced up and flashed the girl a huge smile and a wave. Kensy shrank down in her seat and turned the other way.

Max walked to the opposite end of the pitch. Fortunately, he'd paid close attention to the earlier innings and now stood with his bat poised, waiting for Van to hit the ball.

"Just breathe, Max," Fitz whispered. "If I can do this, so can you."

The bowler ran in beside them and unleashed a bouncer. Van swung and hooked the ball to square leg. "Run!" he yelled, as Max hotfooted it to the other end of the pitch. Max turned to run back as he really didn't want to be on strike, but Van held up his hand, motioning for him to stay put.

Max took a deep breath and stared down the bowler, who was rubbing the red ball against his white pants. "You're gone," the boy mouthed, before he took a longer-than-usual run-up and unleashed the ball, which whizzed past the stumps and into the wicketkeeper's gloves. Max had swung and missed and was feeling rattled.

The wicketkeeper slapped his gloves together and crouched behind the stumps. "This one's ours," he snarled.

"Don't worry, Max, you can do it!" Kensy shouted.

This time Max kept his eyes on the ball. The bowler took his run-up and sent it hurtling down the pitch. Max swung and connected. The hollow sound of bat on ball was glorious. The ball sailed into the air and over the fielders' heads toward the boundary. Max couldn't believe his eyes as it came down on the other side of the fence. Six! The team went wild, clapping and cheering. Kensy was on her feet screaming too.

"Well done, Max," Jaco yelled.

Van gave him a nod and a grin.

Max connected with the next ball too. This time they got three runs and Van was back on strike. The score began to climb and it looked as if the horror run of wickets had come to an end. Before anyone knew it, there were three balls left and the home team needed eight runs to win. Max was back on strike and loving every second.

Kensy felt as though her heart was about to burst through her chest. She was thrilled and terrified for her brother all at the same time. "Come on, Max," she whispered.

They scored two runs off the next ball and then Max walloped a four.

Ellery arrived just in time to see the last delivery. "Are they going to win?" she asked.

"They will if my brother has anything to do with it," Kensy said, hoping her confidence was not misplaced.

The boys in the grandstand were going wild. "Go, Max! You've got this!" they yelled, then started chanting "Wentworth" followed by three loud claps. Max was trying to block out the noise and concentrate on the ball. They needed two runs to win and it was all down to him. It was sort of like a dream, although he suspected that, if he missed, the situation might turn into something akin to a nightmare.

Max gripped the bat tightly and watched as the final ball sped toward him. It bounced up, and he smashed it into the outfield. One boy ran backward and leapt high, but the ball clipped the tips of his fingers and flew over the fence. Six! Max and Van took off toward each other on the pitch, high-fiving and hugging. Wentworth Grammar had won the match.

"Woo-hoo!" Kensy was jumping up and down and shouting. Ellery had been swept away in the moment too and was cheering wildly.

The boys shook hands with their opponents and gathered together at the side of the oval to sing the team song. Their spirits were soaring.

"Your brother is amazing," Van said to Kensy as the pair walked into the stand. "He totally saved us."

"Max is good like that," Kensy replied with a wry grin on her face.

"Ah, Kensy's not too bad either," Max said with a nod. It wasn't lost on him that the only reason he'd been out there was because of his sister's ingenuity.

Van looked at the girl and smiled. "She is pretty awesome."

Kensy's cheeks lit up like a Christmas tree.

Ellery rolled her eyes. "Do you still want to come to our place for a swim when we get home?" she asked.

That was about the last thing Kensy wanted to do, but she could hardly say no. "Sure," she said, "that would be fun."

Ellery looked at her watch. "Ugh, I don't know where Mum's got to. She's supposed to be picking us up. I've tried calling, but she's not answering."

Fitz joined the children. "You could have a lift back with us if you like," he offered.

Kensy had felt bad about not catching the ferry home with Curtis. She'd quietly mentioned her new dance class to him at the end of the day and he said that was fine and he'd see them in the morning. But she could sense his disappointment – and if not his, then her own.

"Max, could I have a word?" Jaco De Vere called. "How would you like a spot on the team this weekend? After that show out there, I think we could do with someone like you in the ranks."

Max grinned. He didn't have the heart to tell the man that was the first time he'd ever played a proper competitive game of cricket. It looked like Fitz wasn't going to be the only one studying the rules over the coming days.

CHAPTER 23

NRHHRMT

"Have you been able to get hold of Mum?" Ellery asked. She glanced across at her brother, who was sitting on the other side of Max in the back of the Land Rover. Kensy was in the front, having raced to jump in first and put some distance between her and Van.

"No, she hasn't picked up my calls or replied to my texts," the boy said. "She's probably at the beautician or something and can't get to her phone. You know what Mum's like."

But Ellery knew that wasn't what their mother was like at all. She always took their calls and texts and she'd never missed a day of picking them up from school.

A marked police car and another two vehicles had just pulled up at the curb outside the Chalmers' house. A tall man in a smart suit and a young woman in a formfitting cream dress and matching heels greeted the officers – two uniformed and four who were likely plainclothes detectives – at the front gate.

Ellery opened the door and leapt out of the car as it was rolling to a stop. Van followed suit but not before thanking Fitz for the lift and saying goodbye to Kensy and Max. The children's father looked over and gave a wave, then jogged down the path toward them.

Fitz tensed, his grip tightening on the steering wheel. "Kids, you'd better pray this disguise is effective or we're in trouble," he muttered, before lowering his window. "Hi there," he said.

"Dash Chalmers," the man said by way of introduction, offering his hand.

Fitz noted that Dash hadn't lost his

American accent at all despite living in Australia for years now. "Gerry Grey," Fitz said, searching the man's face for any sign of recognition. "I'm the new assistant cricket coach and PE teacher at Wentworth Grammar."

Dash nodded. "Thanks for bringing the children home," he said. "I'm afraid there's been an incident."

"I hope everything's okay," Fitz said, counting on the fact that Dash was still as big a talker as he'd always been.

"Not really. My, uh, my wife's disappeared," Dash said.

Kensy and Max looked at each other.

"Are you certain?" Fitz asked. "The children seemed to think she might just be running late from an appointment."

Dash shook his head. "She's never missed picking them up from school, and the police have tracked her phone to a remote location west of the Blue Mountains. It was lying on the side of the road. Her car was found a few miles away, but there was no sign of Tinsley."

"That's terrible," Fitz said. "I'm so sorry. Can we do anything to help?"

Dash's face began to crumple. "It's just . . . I don't even want to think about what could have happened. She's the love of my life and the children are her whole world."

"I'm sure the police will do everything they can," Fitz said, as a convoy of news trucks drove into the street. Reporters and cameramen spilled out of the vehicles, heading for the house.

"Mr. Chalmers," one of the police officers called. "We need to get inside and set up for the press conference."

The man turned and gave a nod.

"I mean it. Please let us know if there's anything we can do," Fitz said. "I can take the children to school in the morning or drop them back afterward. Or they could stay with us tonight?"

"My assistant, Lucy, is going to look after them this evening – she took the children up to the house just now. They can catch the ferry in the morning, but perhaps you can bring them home? They've got after-school activities.

That's always been Tinsley's job," Dash said. "I've got a hectic day of meetings tomorrow."

"No problem," Fitz said, thinking it was strange that Dash was worried about a busy workday when it seemed that his wife had very likely met with foul play.

Kensy and Max were wondering the same thing. The whole situation was bizarre. They watched Dash walk back to the property and the gates close behind him.

"Okay – so what's really going on?" Max asked, leaning between the two front seats.

"Good question," Fitz said, his mouth set in a grim line. He turned the ignition and drove home.

"I thought we were supposed to be watching the kids and now it's their mother who's gone missing. What's that about?" Kensy said, her brows knitted together. "The message this morning mentioned that she was making a move soon, but suddenly she's disappeared – that doesn't make any sense at all."

Max spotted Curtis standing on his front porch. The boy gave a wave as the car pulled into the driveway. The twins waved back before the garage door opened and Fitz parked the car inside.

"We should go and say hello," Max said. Kensy had told him what happened at lunchtime and how horrible she'd felt about it.

"All right, but don't be long," Fitz said, opening the driver's door. "The news will be on in a little while and I think Dash is going to be front and center. We need to see what the police are sharing."

Kensy and Max dumped their bags at the bottom of the staircase and yelled a quick hello to Song before heading out the front door. They peered around the dividing wall to see if Curtis was still there.

"Hi," Max said, noticing that the lad had his backpack on and looked as if he was about to go somewhere. "Where are you off to?"

"I saw some news trucks driving down Blues Point Road. Thought I'd take a look," Curtis said. Unlike yesterday, he didn't immediately extend an invitation for the twins to join him.

"They're outside the Chalmers' place," Kensy said, hoping that by giving him some information he'd feel a little better toward her.

"How do you know that?" Curtis asked.

Kensy explained that they'd dropped Van and Ellery at home as the police and news crews had arrived.

"I always knew there was something weird going on in that family," Curtis said, clicking his tongue.

For the first time, Max wondered if the boy might actually have some useful information.

"What do you mean?" Kensy asked.

"Just stuff," Curtis said with a shrug.

Clearly, he wasn't about to be drawn on whatever it was he'd gathered. "Oh, okay," Kensy said, taking a different tack. She bet Curtis would be more inclined to tell her if she pretended she wasn't interested.

"We'd better let you go then," Max said, tuning into his sister's wavelength.

Kensy opened the front door and was about to step inside when Curtis piped up.

"Do you want to come with me?" he asked.

Kensy grinned. "You bet!"

And with that, Kensy and Curtis scampered down the path while Max stayed behind to watch the press conference under the guise of too much homework. He told Fitz where she'd gone and they both agreed it was probably a good idea to keep an eye on the Chalmers' house – and perhaps Kensy could teach Curtis some surveillance techniques. Although, given the lad's fervor for spying, there was a possibility that could go either way.

CHAPTER 24

HZUV ZMW HLFMW

Kensy finished brushing her teeth and spat into the sink. "It's horrible what's happened to Mrs. Chalmers," she said, looking at her brother in the mirror. She wiped her mouth with the back of her hand. "Van and Ellery must be worried sick about her."

Max nodded. "We know what that feels like."

Unfortunately, there was nothing of note to report after Kensy's stakeout with Curtis. She had learned more about the boy's bag of gadgets, which included a pretty impressive collection of skeleton keys she was fairly certain had never been used, a huge magnifying glass, binoculars, his notebook and invisible-ink pen, a length of rope, a water bottle and a survival kit. As for the press conference, the news bulletin had only shown Dash appealing for information and wiping his eyes with a handkerchief. There were no material leads – at least none that the police were sharing.

"Did you realize Mum and Dad have been gone for over three months now?" Max said, cleaning his toothbrush and replacing it in the holder.

"Three months, two days and sixteen hours." Kensy opened the medicine cabinet in search of aloe vera. "I can't stop thinking about them since Mrs. Chalmers' disappearance. The whole situation has been playing over and over in my head, but there are too many missing pieces. So, our grandparents were supposedly killed in a botched robbery twelve years ago, but they weren't. Then Mum and Dad and Fitz went missing in the fake plane crash, but that was a lie. I wonder if Hector and Marisol knew about that. Do you think our grandparents got a message to Mum and Dad? Or did Mum and Dad discover something that suggested our grandparents aren't dead?"

Max frowned. "Given how often we moved, it would have been impossible to send a letter – unless it took years to reach Mum."

"And they never even made it to Africa, although Fitz said they were in the Maldives at one point. Something must have happened there, or on the way there, for them to know Hector and Marisol were still alive," Kensy said, rubbing the soothing lotion onto her sunburned arms. "Have you been talking to Carlos at all?"

Max glanced at his sister in the mirror, then spat into the sink. "Um, yeah, just the other night. Why? You'd better not have blabbed to Autumn."

"Why would you immediately assume that?" Kensy retorted. "Autumn called a little while ago on the video link. I gather you probably knew that she and Carlos have been doing some investigations of their own about the house explosion. Apparently, there are no fingerprints and the lab hasn't been able to trace where the ingredients of the bomb came from either. She knew about the missing CCTV footage too."

Max's eyebrows jumped up. "Wow, she's amazing."

"I'm pretty sure that feeling is mutual," Kensy quipped.

The pair was interrupted by Fitz calling them from downstairs. "Kids, you might want to come and take a look at this!" he yelled.

Kensy dropped the bottle of aloe vera onto the vanity and ran out of the bathroom with Max behind her. They found Song and Fitz standing in front of the television in the family room. There on the screen was Dash Chalmers with his arm wrapped around his wife and news crews clamoring to get close to them.

"They found her already?" Max asked. "That's so unlikely. Statistically speaking, ninety-nine percent of missing people turn up and eighty-five percent of them appear within the first week, but when it comes to abductions, only around fifty percent of people are found inside thirty days."

"Someone's been paying attention in class," Fitz said with a grin.

Kensy sank down on the sofa. "What a relief."

The footage looked to be out in the bush somewhere and Mrs. Chalmers had an angry red mark on her forehead and a bandage on her left arm.

"Thank you all for your concern," Dash said to the camera as they walked toward an ambulance. A team of paramedics flanked the couple on either side and there were police officers too.

"Do you know who was responsible for your wife's disappearance?" a reporter asked.

Dash looked straight down the barrel of the camera lens. "At this stage, there are no leads, but rest assured I will be working with the police to bring whoever did this to justice."

"Was it a kidnapping? Did you pay a ransom?" two reporters asked over the top of one another.

"Has this got anything to do with The Chalmers Corporation? It has just been named the most powerful pharmaceutical company in the world," another journalist asked.

"Look, that's all in the hands of the police," Dash said. "Now, please, my wife needs to rest and we have to get home to our children. Thank you all for your concern. We've been overwhelmed with support, but, for now, I ask that you give us our privacy so my wife can recover from her ordeal."

"Did you see that?" Kensy said, leaning forward.

"What?" Max asked.

Kensy rewound the footage and hit pause. "That there!" she said, jiggling on the spot. "See that look on Mrs. Chalmers' face and how she pulls away when Dash leans in closer? Don't you think that's weird?"

"That is a very impressive observation, Miss Kensington," Song said.

Fitz nodded. "Yes, well done, Kens."

"I have a very bad feeling about this," Kensy said. "There's something off about the whole idea that she's planning to take the children away. I mean, maybe she has a good reason."

"You're right that it doesn't add up," Max said. "What do you think, Fitz?"

"Tinsley looked absolutely terrified," he said. "Not like a woman with a plan, that's for sure."

"Well, as much as I'd prefer not to, I think we'd better work out a way to spend a lot of time with those kids over the coming days," Kensy said. "Before anyone else disappears."

CHAPTER 25

NLIV GSZM VCKVXGVW

Overnight, a thunderstorm had growled and crackled across the city, blowing away the oppressive heat that had been building for days. This morning the sky was a cerulean blue with a salty freshness in the air. Curtis had been waiting for the twins at the front gate and there was a spring in their steps as the three of them walked to the ferry, chattering about the events of the previous evening. It had come as something of a surprise to see Van and Ellery there on the wharf too, given the circumstances. Seizing the opportunity,

Max hurried over to chat with Van while Kensy made an excuse to Curtis that she needed to ask Ellery about their dance classes. Of course, she was actually eager to find out how their mother was.

The harbor was like a millpond this morning. Curtis stood on his own, surveying the scene. There were the usual morning commuters, but one man he didn't know was taking lots of pictures on his phone. He would have looked like any other tourist, dressed as he was in a T-shirt, cargo shorts and sandals, except that Curtis was certain every snap of the harbor also contained either Ellery or Van.

"Excuse me," the lad said. "Would you like me to get a picture with you in it?"

The man frowned. "What? No, thank you."

Kensy looked up and spotted the pair. She wondered what Curtis was doing.

"Well, I think you should stop taking photos of my friends," the boy demanded loudly, garnering everyone's attention.

The man looked aghast. "Excuse me?"

Ellery's ears pricked. "Why is Curtis Pepper

talking about us to that guy?" she asked in a peevish tone.

"I'll find out," Kensy said, and hurried over to Curtis. "Have you been taking photos of schoolchildren?" Kensy asked the man. "You could get into a lot of trouble for doing that, you know."

A deep-red blush crept up the man's neck to his cheeks. "Please mind your own business. I can assure you I'm not interested in schoolkids," he snapped, before dropping his phone into his daypack and stalking off to the other end of the wharf.

By now the ferry had arrived and the passengers were beginning to board. Max sat with Van halfway down the cabin. He'd managed to ask the boy a couple of questions about his mother, but there wasn't anything more to tell than what had already been aired on the news. Apparently, she was fine and Van said she didn't even seem that upset about what had happened, which Max found very surprising.

Ellery sat at the back of the boat. She pulled out a book and buried her head inside, clearly not keen to talk to anyone this morning. Kensy, meanwhile, waited until the man on the wharf had boarded and she and Curtis scooted into the seats immediately behind him.

"I think he must be working for the press," Curtis whispered. "He's probably going to sell those photos to some dodgy magazine."

Kensy nodded. She'd been thinking the same thing. "I've got an idea," she said, a grin forming on her lips. "You distract him so I can get hold of his phone."

The boy's eyes widened. "Distract him? How?"

"You know – make a fuss," Kensy said. "Just do what you can to get his attention for a moment."

Curtis suddenly felt ill despite remembering his pill this morning. "What are you going to do?"

"Never mind that," Kensy said. "Seriously, if you have aspirations of espionage, you need to do what I say, okay?"

Curtis gulped. There was something about Kensy's manner that made him feel a little bit scared and a little bit excited at the same time. He took a deep breath and sprang into action, tapping the man on the shoulder. It was a game his father played with him all the time until he got wise to it, which sadly he still wasn't always, even after years of being tricked. The man spun around as Kensy leaned over the top of the seat and unzipped his daypack, digging around and grabbing what she was after.

"What do you want?" he fumed.

"Um, to apologize for before," Curtis said. "It was wrong of me to assume you were up to something."

The man looked at Curtis quizzically. "Okay, whatever. Don't worry about it." He flicked his hand and turned to face the front.

As the ferry chugged into Circular Quay, Kensy quickly transferred some pictures of Van and Ellery and more of their house and their father in his car to her own device before she deleted them permanently from the man's phone. She might have gotten a few extras, but there wasn't time to check.

Curtis looked at Kensy in awe. "What are you going to do with it now?" he whispered.

"Watch and learn, Curtis Pepper," the girl said with a glint in her eye. She really shouldn't have been doing any of this in front of the lad, but given his penchant for surveillance, she couldn't help herself. Besides, if she didn't do it now with his help, she'd miss her opportunity. Kensy waited for the man to walk ahead of her. She then went to drop the device into his unzipped bag, except at that very moment he pulled it up on his shoulder and the phone clattered to the floor. Kensy was on it in a flash and picked it up just as the man turned around to see what the noise was.

"What are you doing with that?" he said, spotting the phone in Kensy's hand.

"It fell out of your bag," Kensy replied innocently. "I was only trying to help."

"Oh, thank you," he said with a smile. He dropped it into his shorts pocket.

Beads of perspiration trickled down Curtis's forehead as they walked toward the gangplank and onto the wharf.

"Max," Kensy called to her brother, who was dawdling along with Van. Ellery was further behind them. "Hurry up!" Kensy nodded toward the man, whose face told the story that he'd just realized he'd been duped by an eleven-year-old.

"You have no idea what you've done!" he shouted, sprinting toward Kensy and Curtis. But Max and Van had started after them and Van grabbed his sister along the way. They all charged past him, catching up to Kensy and Curtis. "You lousy kids!" he shouted.

The five children sprinted along the concourse and turned right into Macquarie Street. A garbage truck hurtled toward the roundabout near the Opera House and blocked the man's path, allowing them time to put some distance between them.

"Who was that guy?" Van puffed.

"Let's just say that you and Ellery were probably going to be on some dodgy news site in a few minutes if Kensy hadn't intervened," Curtis panted.

Van gazed at Kensy in admiration. "Cool."

"It was nothing – and I shouldn't have done it, but he'd taken pictures of the two of you and your dad as well when he must have been leaving for work this morning. I'm guessing you don't really want to be splashed all over the media," Kensy said.

"Thank you," Van said with a grin, while his sister didn't utter a word. Apparently, the idea of being paparazzi fodder didn't bother Ellery nearly as much.

The children ran until they couldn't see the man anymore.

Van almost knocked Curtis sideways as he maneuvered himself next to Kensy. "I can't believe you did that for us. What if he'd caught you in the act? He could have called the police."

Kensy shrugged. "He did catch me, but I suspect he might not have been exactly on the right side of the law himself."

"So how was yesterday?" Van asked as they walked up the street. He looked at her and smiled. "We never really got to talk."

"It was fine," Kensy said, her cheeks blazing and not just from the morning sun.

Max could feel his sister's discomfort from where he was standing on the other side of Curtis. After the earlier kerfuffle, Ellery had run ahead to join her friends. The children turned into the gate. Kensy was growing hotter by the second and couldn't wait to get to their air-conditioned classroom. As they neared the buildings, Van was quickly set upon by his friends, who wanted to know if he was okay.

"I told you he likes you," Curtis said as he and Kensy walked on to their homerooms.

"For goodness' sake," Kensy said, holding up a hand in protest. "Stop speaking!"

"I thought you'd be flat–"

"Zip it," Kensy said, and mimed zipping her lips shut.

"But . . ."

"I'm warning you, Curtis." Kensy's face was the color of beets. She spun around and spied Max laughing at her from across the quadrangle. "And you can put a sock in it too!" she yelled, then turned on her heel and charged inside the building.

CHAPTER 26

Z SLIIRW YFHRMVHH

"*Please* be extremely careful with those vials," Hector said to whoever was on the other side of the one-way glass panel. He wanted to tell them that the virus he and Marisol had been working on for the past few months had the potential to kill millions if it fell into the wrong hands. But what was the point? It was already in the wrong hands and, besides, at the same time they created the disease they developed the cure. It would go out when the time was right, when whoever had unleashed all that pain and suffering was ready to make millions from the antidote.

Their new laboratory was state of the art, but, as always, their single computer could access scientific data and nothing else. When Hector had attempted to find an open path to the internet, the machine automatically locked and they were frozen out for a day. There was no point trying again.

Surveillance cameras covered every square inch of the laboratory, monitoring their every move, and Hector was certain it was the same in their living quarters at the end of the long corridor.

Whoever was in charge was clearly not going to make the same mistake twice, as they had not had any physical or verbal contact with anyone since the move.

Hector still felt a creeping dread whenever he thought about Miguel. He had taken such huge risks to help them. Marisol had blamed herself for involving the young man, but Hector reminded her that it was Miguel who had come to them, desperate for a cure for his mother. In return, he had tried a number of times to contact their daughter. He had helped them for almost a year, then one morning not long ago, they awoke in this new place and Miguel was gone. They could only hope that he had managed to get away from whoever was at the helm of this horrid business.

CHAPTER 27

HFIEVROOZMXV

The rest of the week at school was so busy the twins barely had time to think. Between classes and choir rehearsals, cricket practice and dance lessons, Kensy and Max were beginning to think life in London, even with all of their Pharos activities, was a lot quieter. Perhaps it was because there was a never-ending array of extracurricular activities on top of their regular schoolwork, not to mention daily debriefings and training sessions with Fitz and Song. The twins had both made firm friends with their targets, though Kensy was still grumbling about drawing the short straw with Ellery. The girl was a nasty piece of work and grumpier than a wombat with a toothache most of the time.

At least Max's inclusion in the cricket team was proving fruitful. The twins had managed to wangle an invitation to stay at the Chalmers' farm in the Southern Highlands for the weekend after the match at Bradman Oval, and Fitz along with them.

They spent several afternoons at the Chalmers' residence too, which was good for surveillance but bad for Curtis because Ellery took any opportunity to make it patently clear that he wasn't welcome. Kensy could have strangled the girl when, on their way home on the ferry, she invited her and Max over right in front of the lad. Kensy suggested that Curtis might like to have a swim too, but Ellery just ignored her. Curtis had mumbled something about a music lesson and that he'd catch up with them later. It made Kensy think of Misha and how hard it must have been for her to pretend to be besties with

Lola Lemmler all that time — there were some sacrifices being a trainee agent that she didn't enjoy at all.

"I need a drink," Ellery whined following their second game of Marco Polo. "Mummy!"

"I'll go," Max said, leaping at the opportunity to have a word with Tinsley Chalmers. He toweled himself dry, then wandered into the kitchen, where the woman had just finished pouring four large tumblers of ice water. "Can I take them out for you?" he asked.

Tinsley jumped, almost knocking over a glass. "Silly me," she said, smiling. "Thanks, Max. I wish Van and Ellery would take some cues from you and your sister — you both have such lovely manners. I imagine your mother must be very proud." The woman grimaced. "Sorry, I didn't mean to be so insensitive."

"It's okay. I know Mum would be if she was here." It wasn't a lie. His mother prided herself on having taught the twins to be helpful. "How are you feeling?" he asked. The bandage on the woman's arm was gone, although he could detect a hint of the bruise

224

on Tinsley's forehead despite her attempt to disguise it with makeup.

"Oh, I'm fine," she said.

Max wasn't convinced. Tinsley might have seemed okay on the outside, but she had no doubt suffered a harrowing experience and was bound to be rattled. "Are the police any closer to finding out who was responsible?" he asked.

Tinsley shook her head. "I don't think so. They took DNA samples from under my fingernails, but there weren't any matches with the police database. I was bound and gagged on the floor in the back. Whoever took me never said a word. We drove for hours with the radio on – that's how I kept track of the time and I knew we'd gone quite a long way when the stations began to crackle and the driver had to find another one."

"You must have been terrified," Max said. "Did you think you'd been kidnapped for ransom? I mean, your husband is in charge of such a big business – people must get to know things."

"Oh gosh, it's lucky I wasn't – I'd probably still be out there," she quipped, then seemed to immediately regret it. "Just kidding. I was pretty sure it was a carjacking – there were no phone calls or anything like that."

Max looked at her. For someone who was supposed to be scheming to take her children away, she looked more like a wounded animal and a frightened one at that. The woman's phone rang, surprising them both. Tinsley took a deep breath before answering.

"Hello, Lucy. Yes, I'm fine, and you really don't have to keep checking up on me . . . Oh. That would be lovely, thank you." Tinsley hung up and rolled her eyes. "My husband's assistant must have called twenty times since the incident and she just asked me to have lunch with her tomorrow – Dash is out of town for a couple of days and he's probably told her to keep an eye on me. Anyway, you don't need to hear my tales of woe, Max – you're a very sweet young man to ask."

"It's okay, Mrs. Chalmers, we all need to talk to somebody from time to time," the boy said, and walked back out to the patio with the tray of drinks.

On their way home, Max told Kensy about his conversation.

"So, you think she's scared?" Kensy said. "I know she's constantly monitored – there are cameras everywhere in that house. Some of them are obvious, but there are hidden ones too. Did you see the porcelain dog on the mantelpiece in the lounge? Its eyes follow you everywhere. I was glad I realized almost straightaway or else I might have been accused of snooping once whoever reviews the footage notices."

"I don't know if she was joking when she said she was glad it wasn't a kidnapping or she'd probably still be out there. It doesn't add up. Dash seems to adore the woman," Max said. The twins trudged up the hill in silence for a few minutes before turning the corner.

"I love all this stuff, Max," Kensy said. "I know I shouldn't because there's a possibility that someone's in danger, but don't you find it just a little bit thrilling?"

"Or a lot." Max smiled. "I feel the same way. I think it must in our blood, don't you?"

As they crossed the road into Waiwera Street, they noticed Curtis on the sidewalk. He had a towel around his shoulders and was wearing a pair of jelly sandals.

"Hey!" Kensy called to the boy. "Where are you going?"

Curtis sighed and wiped his sweaty brow. "I was thinking about having a swim at the North Sydney pool, but I don't know if I can face the walk – it's so hot again."

"You can come over to our place, if you like – we won't be doing laps, but you can cool off," Kensy said.

Curtis grinned. "Thanks, that'd be awesome."

Max nudged his sister. "You know you're not as bad as people say."

"Gee, thanks. You'd better run and check that Song isn't in the middle of something Curtis shouldn't see," she said. "I'll stall him for a second."

Max nodded. "Good thinking," he said, and sprinted toward their house.

CHAPTER 28

XSVIIB GIVV UZIN

Saturday morning dawned bright and blue as the children and Fitz set off early for the Highlands. Song was staying back in Sydney and planned to keep an eye on the Chalmers' residence. Kensy and Max had suggested he might like to orchestrate a meeting with their housekeeper, Rosa. Kensy had deliberately left her towel there on Friday afternoon so he'd have an excuse to drop round and snoop.

"This is a pretty place," Kensy said as Fitz turned into a tree-lined street and pulled up outside the Bradman Museum.

"The Highlands are about as close to England as you're going to get in Australia," the man said. He scratched at his turkey neck, but it did nothing to relieve the itch underneath.

Max hopped out of the car and called to Van. The Chalmers had just parked a few spots further down.

"I can't believe I have to spend the whole day with Ellery," Kensy moaned, watching the girl hop out of their car.

Fitz grinned. "Gee, Kens, anyone would think the poor girl was the devil incarnate, hearing the way you speak about her."

"You said it, not me." Kensy squeezed her eyes and groaned. "She does my head in. And next time she's rude to Curtis, I swear I'm going to punch her in the nose."

"Probably not a good idea, Kens," Fitz said with a wink. He fetched his rule book from the glove compartment and shut the door.

Kensy rolled her eyes and almost jumped out of her skin when there was a thump on her window. Ellery's long dark hair was pulled back into a high ponytail by a big white bow which perfectly matched her white jeans, white sneakers and white T-shirt with the word "Angel" emblazoned across the front in silver sparkles.

"Hurry up! Mum's taking us to the shops!" the girl yelled, rapping on the window again.

"Angel? That's a joke," Kensy muttered before exiting the car and plastering a huge smile on her face. "Hi! You look amazing!" she said, immediately wishing she hadn't because that was just mean.

"Hi, Kensy!" Van called loudly. "Love your boots."

Kensy looked down at the pair of trendy boots Song had bought the day before. He'd arrived home with what looked to be half the shop to make sure the kids were appropriately dressed for their weekend in the country. "Thanks," she said, flushing bright red. "I, um, love your cricket cap."

Max chuckled, shaking his head. "Wow, you two are really something."

"Not another word," Kensy grouched, and slunk off to join Ellery at her car.

"See you later, Tins," Dash said. "Remember to pick up some of that washed-rind goat brie from the deli. You know how much I love it."

"Of course," Tinsley murmured. How could she forget? The last time she'd missed it on the grocery list, he'd carried on like a petulant three-year-old whose favorite toy had been left behind.

The girls hopped into Tinsley's car and headed into town. They shopped at the supermarket then the butcher, the florist and the bakery, with a final stop at Ellery's favorite stationery store. Loaded with supplies, they were soon on the road, passing through Moss Vale and Sutton Forest. Before they reached the village of Exeter, they turned left into the poplar-lined drive of a property called Cherry Tree Farm. Kensy thought it sounded like something from a storybook. When they finally reached the house, which was set back at least half a mile from the road, and surrounded by high hedges and mature trees, she felt as if she'd fallen into those very pages.

"Here we are," Tinsley said with a smile. She pulled up at the garage, which was located around the back of the rambling Colonial mansion. The charming two-story house was built of cream stone with wide verandas wrapping around both floors. The upstairs balcony railings resembled the lacelike icing on a wedding cake and the building was topped by a gray slate roof. The garden was equally stunning with its topiary roses and perfect hedges bordering lush green lawns. It reminded Kensy a little of Alexandria except on a much smaller scale, and the house couldn't have been as old either.

"What a beautiful place," she declared.

"I can only agree," Tinsley said as she opened the car door and hopped out. "It's very special."

"Do you get to come here often?" Kensy asked.

"Not as much as we'd like. It's silly, really. It's only a couple of hours from the city, but we never seem to have the time." The woman yawned widely. "Oh, pardon me. We had a very late night."

"I need to pee," Ellery announced and scampered off to the house.

"Were you out?" Kensy asked. She walked around to the back of the car with Tinsley.

The woman nodded and opened the tailgate. "Yes, at a fundraiser. I thought Dash might have changed his mind after . . ."

"After what happened this week?" Kensy said. "I can imagine there were lots of people wanting to know how you were and asking silly questions." The girl picked up a couple of grocery bags and Tinsley gathered several more.

"It was horrible," Tinsley admitted. "I didn't especially want to go. People meant well – except the ones gossiping in the corners. The Chalmers Corporation is one of the major sponsors, so we couldn't get out of it and, besides, no one likes a party more than my husband."

Together, Kensy and Tinsley unloaded the car, making several trips to get everything. Conveniently, by the time Ellery returned, they were done. Considering half the bags belonged to her, it hardly seemed fair. The white country kitchen at the back of the house had an acre of marble countertops with the most massive island in the center. There was an adjoining open-plan family room, which, in spite of its size, was homey and welcoming. It played host to plaid armchairs, an overstuffed navy couch, rugs, cushions and an array of artwork as well as a huge fireplace. Ellery took Kensy on a tour of the rest of the house while Tinsley set about making lunch. In addition to the kitchen and family room, the lower level comprised a formal lounge and dining room, a study, powder room and laundry, and a guest bedroom suite.

"Now I'll show you my room," Ellery said, bounding up the main staircase. "It's way nicer than my Sydney bedroom even though I hardly ever get to use it."

Kensy could only agree. The space was enormous, with a life-sized dappled-gray rocking horse in one corner, an impressive doll's house that looked as if it was for eyes only, and two pretty iron bedsteads with floral linen. The wide cedar floorboards were partly covered by a plush rug. Kensy ran her finger along Ellery's bookshelf, which was populated with lots of her favorites, when her wrist vibrated.

"Seriously, now?" she muttered.

Ellery stopped ferreting about in the wardrobe. "Did you say something?"

"I was just wondering if there's a bathroom nearby." Kensy glanced around for a pen and spotted one on Ellery's desk.

"Through there." The girl pointed at a door in the corner of the room. Trouble was, the desk was at the opposite end, near the door to the hallway.

"Is there one a little further away?" Kensy asked.

Ellery wrinkled her nose. "Why?"

Kensy racked her brain for a reason. "My tummy feels a bit funny and I don't want you to hear any explosions or smell anything nasty," she said, dying inside.

Ellery blanched. "There's a powder room at the end of the hall."

"Thanks!" Kensy spun around and flew past

the desk, where she swiped the pen without Ellery noticing. She sped along the hallway, quickly locating the room she was looking for, then sat down on the closed lid and pulled the toilet paper from the roll onto her lap. She did her best to translate the dots and dashes, but the Chalmers must have had the softest toilet tissue in the world. The pen kept piercing through. Kensy willed the sequence to repeat, but it stopped for good. "No!" she moaned, far louder than she'd intended.

"Are you okay in there?" Ellery called from the other side of the door.

"I'm fine," Kensy replied. She stared miserably at the massacred length of toilet paper in her hands.

"Would you like me to get Mum?"

"No, give me a few minutes. I think it'll pass," Kensy said, wishing the girl would just buzz off. She made the loudest farting noise she could with her mouth and hoped that would do the trick.

"Eww. I'll be downstairs."

Kensy bit back a giggle and put the sheet of toilet tissue on the vanity top. She began to write the first letters when Tinsley tapped on the door and asked if she was all right.

"Well, I'm going to sit out here and wait just to be sure," the woman replied when Kensy assured her she was fine. "Van once had a twisted bowel and ended up in the emergency room. I don't want the same happening to you."

Honestly, no one had ever cared this much about Kensy's toilet habits before. She decided to translate the coded message later. She folded up the piece of toilet paper and stuffed it into the pocket of her jeans, then flushed the toilet and washed her hands.

"Are you sure you're all right?" Tinsley asked when Kensy emerged. She stood up and walked toward the girl, concern etched into her features.

"I feel much better," Kensy said, flashing the woman a smile. "Actually, I'm starving. Sometimes I just get a grumbly tummy – it's embarrassing, but I suppose we all have our problems."

Tinsley tilted her head to one side. "How do you mean?"

"Everyone has something wrong with them at times, like F– I mean, Dad – has dodgy knees even though he likes to pretend he's still twenty and can ski like an Olympian," Kensy said, berating herself for almost mentioning Fitz's name.

"Yes, I suppose you're right," Tinsley said. "Dash has awful allergies. He should carry an EpiPen, but he usually forgets to take it with him."

Kensy suddenly had an overwhelming urge to sneeze. She reached into her pocket and pulled out a tissue, only just catching it. Then, with a sinking feeling she realized it wasn't a tissue at all. She'd just snotted on her parents' latest communication. She needed to check it and fast before the whole thing was a blur of ink. "Sorry, not quite better yet," Kensy said, and dashed back to the toilet, slamming the door behind her.

There was no time to lose. She unfurled the tissue and grabbed another to try to complete the translation, but it was hopeless. All she was able to decipher was "ATARA," which was clearly missing some letters.

Fighting back tears, Kensy flushed the toilet again and washed her hands, then stuffed both lengths of tissue into her pocket. She couldn't believe how badly she'd messed up. It wasn't lost on her that this message from her parents could have been the most important one yet. Kensy reached for the handle, then paused. She took a deep breath and brushed at her eyes. Hopefully, Max had been able to jot part, if not all, of it down. Who knew what was at stake?

CHAPTER 29

GRNV GL GZOP

It seemed Mrs. Chalmers had procured far more than just a few humble sandwiches for their lunch. A feast of quiches, baguettes, sausage rolls and just about every cold meat and sandwich filling imaginable was spread across the island. In addition, a chocolate cake and a passion fruit tart were each housed under glass domes. Kensy licked her lips and sighed. She couldn't possibly fit in another thing. She wiped her hands and asked Ellery if she wanted to go for a walk – anything to distract her from her thoughts for a little while – but the girl wasn't remotely interested.

"It's too hot," Ellery complained. "And the flies are terrible."

Tinsley stood up and began clearing things away. "Perhaps you and Kensy would like to go for a swim then," she suggested.

"Daddy said the pool heater is broken and the water will be like ice," the girl moped.

Tinsley gave Kensy a tight smile. "What about a board game?"

"Boring!" Ellery rolled her eyes and rested her chin in her hands. She spotted a lone ant scurrying between the plates and crushed the creature with her index finger.

Kensy glanced at the kitchen clock, praying that Max and Fitz would be home soon. Ellery was really getting on her nerves and she needed to talk to her brother.

"Well, I'll come for a walk with you," Tinsley said, smiling at Kensy. "Just give me a minute to finish putting all of this away."

Kensy gave the woman a hand while Ellery played a game on her mother's phone.

She was soon distracted by a scratching sound on the other side of the kitchen door and was surprised to see a fat ginger cat pushing its way inside.

"Oh, hello, Meggs," Tinsley said. She put the food she was holding on the counter and bent down to give the cat a rub.

"Is he yours?" Kensy asked, wondering how the creature survived on the farm on its own.

"He's mine," Ellery said, "but Daddy's allergic to the fur, so we had to bring him to live here."

"Our farm manager, Nick, looks after him for us. He lives in a cottage on the other side of the trees," Tinsley explained. "Poor Meggs. He's such a sweet little fellow." The cat purred loudly, as if in agreement. Tinsley disappeared into the pantry and returned with a handful of treats. "Here you go, lovely boy. Just make yourself scarce before Dash gets home."

"Are you sure you don't want to join us?" Tinsley asked.

Ellery made a face. "No, I'm going to watch a movie."

"Suit yourself. But your father won't be very happy if he catches you inside on a day like this," Tinsley warned.

"Whatever." Ellery waved her hand dismissively, her eyes glued to the screen.

"Come on then, Kensy, let's take a walk in the sunshine. I haven't been round the property for so long, it will do me good," the woman said with a somewhat apologetic smile.

Kensy practically ran to the door. Not only was it a relief to have a break from Ellery, she was aware this was the perfect chance to gather more intel from Tinsley. At least she could still do something useful today.

The pair walked through the back garden, which was less formal than the front but with a swimming pool enclosed by a glass fence and an adjoining tennis court with a summer house between the two. There was a shed further beyond and a small herd of black cattle in the paddock. Tinsley chatted away, pointing out various parts of the property.

"The railway line on that side forms one boundary and the road down there is another, and in that direction the land runs for a couple of miles," Tinsley said, turning a circle as she pointed in each direction.

"Are there many trains?" Kensy asked.

"It's the main line between Sydney and Melbourne, so there are quite a few, though they never bother me," Tinsley said, tucking her hair behind her ears.

"There's something comforting about the *clackety-clack*. I grew up near a railway line and it always reassured me that I had somewhere to go. Life wouldn't always be the way it was."

"And is that how it turned out for you?" Kensy asked, sidestepping a fresh cow pie.

Tinsley almost laughed. "Perhaps I should have thought more about what I had instead of always wanting to be somewhere else."

The pair wandered on in silence, down a track that led past a cattle shed and into a forest of tall pine trees. Tinsley stopped and peered through the foliage.

Kensy tried to see what the woman was looking at. "What is it?" she asked.

"Oh, I just don't remember that shed being there," Tinsley said, her brow puckering. "But then again I haven't been out here for ages."

Now that it had been pointed out to her, Kensy could make out a building that was almost obscured by a high cypress hedge.

"Perhaps it's not even on our property," Tinsley pondered aloud. The clatter of an approaching diesel engine filled the air. "I don't recall there being a driveway coming in from that way either. But who knows with Dash. He could have bought the place without even telling me. His business dealings are quite the mystery."

A four-wheel-drive pickup pulled up near the shed and a burly young man jumped out. Kensy thought he must have a full head of curls as he had tufts of hair bursting from under his cap. He walked straight around to the bed and picked up one of several large cardboard boxes.

"Nick!" Tinsley called out, waving.

The man almost lost hold of his cargo as he spun around.

"Sorry, we didn't mean to scare you," Tinsley said, laughing, as they made their way over to him.

The fellow broke into a friendly grin. "Hi, I didn't think you were arriving until later," he said, lowering the box to the ground.

"Ellery refused to watch the boys play cricket and I needed to stock up on supplies," Tinsley explained. She gestured to Kensy. "This is Kensington Grey, one of Van and Ellery's friends."

"Hi," Kensy called and gave a wave.

"Hi there. Ellery must be happy to have someone to play with." He smiled at Kensy and glanced around, looking for the girl.

"Oh, she's watching a movie," Tinsley said. "Said it was too hot for a walk. So, tell me about this shed – is it ours?"

"The shed?" Nick shrugged. "It just houses some farm equipment and a bit of feed, that's all."

"Oh, okay," Tinsley said. "Can we give you a hand? You seem to have rather a full load."

Kensy glanced at the boxes and was

surprised to read the labels: formaldehyde, aluminum salts and thimerosal. They sounded more like pharmaceutical supplies than something required out here, but then again Kensy was the first to admit she didn't know much about farming.

Nick grinned. "Thank you, but I can manage. Mr. Chalmers would be none too happy if I had you doing hard labor." He lifted his cap and ran a hand through his hair. It was hard to miss the deep scratch on the inside of his forearm.

"Ooh, that looks infected," Tinsley said, leaning in to take a closer look. "What on earth did you do to yourself, Nick?"

"Caught it on some barbed wire when I was mending one of the fences," he replied sheepishly. "It's silly, really."

"We should put some antiseptic on it before it gets wor—" Tinsley's face went white. "What time is it?" she asked urgently.

Nick glanced at his watch. "Almost four."

"Oh goodness, we'd better be getting back. Wouldn't want Dash to have to make his own cup of tea now, would we?" Tinsley laughed mirthlessly.

Kensy grinned. "It's okay, Fitz makes a decent brew."

Tinsley frowned at her. "Who?"

"I meant Dad," Kensy said quickly. She could have kicked herself for being so careless. Seriously, if she was in charge of her first Pharos review, she'd be giving herself a big fat fail. "It's a nickname Mum had for him, which we use sometimes. Anyway, should we go?"

Tinsley nodded, clearly distracted. They said goodbye to Nick and hurried back to the main house. As they reached the back garden, Kensy spotted Fitz's Land Rover heading up the drive and broke into a run.

"Did you win?" she asked, panting, as the four of them hopped out.

"It was epic," Max fizzed. His cricket whites were streaked with grass stains and he looked a little pink around the ears.

Van nodded, beaming at the girl. His usually immaculate hair was matted and his whites would need a good soaking too. "We smashed them!"

"I think this calls for a celebration. I hope you have cake," Dash said, looking over at his wife, whose cheeks had regained some color. "Where have you been, darling?"

"Kensy and I went for a walk. You didn't tell me we had a new shed on the northern boundary," Tinsley said, plastering a smile on her lips.

Dash looked at her curiously. "You must be talking about the Davidsons' place," he said, then clapped his hands. "Well, I could murder a cup of tea, and I'm sure the boys would love to give you a blow-by-blow account of their incredible victory."

"They did very well," Fitz said, ruffling Max's hair.

Kensy grinned and gave the man an unexpected hug.

"Are you okay, sweetheart?" he asked, wondering about her spontaneous display of affection.

She nodded and looked up at him, then let

go as quickly as she'd latched on. Kensy nudged her brother's shoulder, and the pair hung back as the others walked toward the house.

"Did you get it?" Kensy whispered.

He shook his head. "It was my turn batting and I had my gloves on. Talk about bad timing. What have I missed?"

Tears sprang to the girl's eyes and she suddenly felt sick to her stomach. "I'm s–"

"Hurry up, you two!" Van called.

Kensy hastily brushed at her face. "I'll tell you later."

As much as they'd rather it didn't, for now, their conversation would just have to wait.

CHAPTER 30

UIFHGIZGRLMH ZMW
IVEVOZGRLMH

Kensy heard the clock downstairs strike midnight when she pushed back the covers and snuck out of the bedroom. She'd been fighting sleep for ages, reading one of Ellery's Nancy Drew mysteries under the covers with a flashlight she'd found in the bedside cabinet. Unfortunately, she hadn't managed a minute alone with Max all evening. The families had enjoyed a barbecue dinner in the pavilion and some lively games of tennis before the children watched a movie together. On their way to bed, the twins had made a plan to meet when everyone was asleep.

Kensy tiptoed along the hallway, hoping that the old house wasn't going to give her up with an inevitable squeaky floorboard. She had almost made it to the staircase when she heard a heated exchange coming from Dash and Tinsley's bedroom.

"I think you need to tell the police," Tinsley said. "They can get his DNA and test it against the sample they got from under my fingernails."

"You're being hysterical. I really don't think there's any chance it was him, but of course I'll call the commissioner when we get back to Sydney," Dash said. "You're going to feel pretty awful, darling, when you realize you're accusing an innocent man."

Kensy heard Tinsley sigh right before their bedroom door swung open. She rolled under a side table, pressing herself flat against the wall as Dash strode past and trotted downstairs. Kensy waited two full minutes before emerging from her hiding spot, reasoning that she could always claim to be fetching a glass of water if she got caught.

Keeping an eye out for Dash, Kensy hot-footed it into the family room. "Max," she whispered. Her feet almost left the ground when he sat up on the couch.

"What took you?" he hissed. After Kensy explained the holdup, she was about to tell him how she'd bungled their parents' message when they heard a voice in the hall.

"Max, are you down here?" Van whispered loudly.

Kensy groaned in frustration. "Seriously?"

"Come on," Max said, grabbing her arm. They hurried into the back hallway, past a wall of framed family photographs. Something caught Max's eye and he stopped. He tugged at her pajama top and pointed to a picture of a young Uncle Rupert with a woman. They were standing together, looking very much in love.

Kensy peered at the photo. "Who's that?" she whispered as Van came through the other door. Max took her hand and they scurried down the front hall, soon realizing there was nowhere to go.

"Max!" Van hissed. "I need to talk to you . . . about Kensy."

"Urgh!" Kensy made a face and shook her head. She opened the door to the powder room and pushed Max inside, closing the door quietly behind them. She was about to explain how she'd messed up everything when they heard Dash's voice loud and clear. It was one of those weird acoustic chambers, where the speaker on the other side of the wall sounded as if they were standing in the same room.

"Tinsley's fine, Mother. She's much happier," Dash said. "No, I don't think there's anything to worry about anymore. She won't be going anywhere."

Kensy nudged her brother much harder than she'd intended, and the boy let out a yelp. Max glared at her. "Are you trying to get caught?" he hissed.

"Sorry, Mum, I have to go," Dash said.

The twins heard his footsteps in the hall. They were waiting for the door handle to turn when he walked back into the study and made another call.

"Five biohazard transport boxes. Nine o'clock Monday morning at the farm," he said, then scoffed as if whoever was on the other end of the line had said something amusing. "If they want to play hardball then they really don't know who they're dealing with. Don't be late. I need to get back to the city before midday."

Kensy was about to tell Max about the note when the floor outside their door squeaked loudly. They heard footsteps and the sound of a door opening.

"Van, what are you doing down here?" Dash asked.

"Max is missing," the boy replied. "I can't find him anywhere."

Kensy grabbed the door handle in case someone tried to open it. Unexpectedly, it came away in her hand and fell with a clatter to the floor. "Oops!" she mouthed.

"Max, is that you?" Van said, turning the handle from the outside. He opened it to find the boy sitting on the toilet seat, looking dazed. "Max," Van said, waving a hand in front of the lad's face.

"He's been sleepwalking." Dash chuckled. He swung Max over his shoulder. "Come on, mate, let's get you back to bed. And remind me to fix that wretched handle tomorrow, Van."

As they spun around in the hallway, Max's eyes fluttered open and looked toward the corner of the ceiling where Kensy had wedged herself between two walls. She was almost in a full splits position, trembling from the effort, and had no idea how much longer she could hold it. When Van closed the door, she landed as softly as she could on the tiles.

Kensy sat on the floor with her back against the wall for the next hour, running through the periodic table of elements over and over in her head in an effort to stay awake. When the clock struck one, Kensy crept along the back hall and was surprised to see Fitz poke his head out of the downstairs guest room to wish her good night. She was too tired to do anything but wave. Back upstairs, Kensy stood outside Max and Van's room. Both boys were snoring. She'd have to wait until tomorrow to tell Max about the message.

CHAPTER 31

NRCVW NVHHZTVH

"Finally!" Kensy exclaimed. "I can't believe we couldn't even get two minutes on our own the whole time we were away." Sparing no detail, the girl explained everything. She pulled the pieces of toilet paper from her pocket and passed them to Max, who had moved into the front passenger seat for the short ride home from where they had just dropped Tinsley and the children in Warung Street. Dash had surprised everyone when he said they wouldn't be heading back until Monday as he had to meet a man about some cattle. Tinsley clearly had no idea about his plans and, given the children had an important choir rehearsal first thing, she didn't fancy a terse phone call from Mr. Thacker or that awful receptionist, Ms. Skidmore, if Van and Ellery weren't there. Fitz had promptly offered them a lift.

"Is that meant to be a dot?" Max asked, squinting at the tissue.

Kensy sighed miserably. "I think there's only one word and I have no idea what it means."

Max fetched a notepad and pen from his daypack and started scribbling. There were a couple of gaps, but it didn't take him long to work out what the word was meant to be. "Kens, of course you know what this means – unless you paid absolutely no attention in our Maori language classes."

Kensy grabbed the notepad and gasped. "Aotearoa! Do you think they could be in New Zealand?" She stared at the neatly printed letters on the page. "How did I not see that?"

Fitz scratched his fake beard. "Don't worry, Kensy – that won't be the last mistake you make in this business. Your father and I almost missed a target entirely when we were newly minted agents and I mixed up the towns of Dunstaple and Barnstaple. Let's just hope Anna and Ed get in contact again soon. At least it sounds as though they're close if they need help."

"I suppose." Kensy's heart swelled inside her chest. "I miss them so much."

"I know you do, sweetheart," Fitz said, looking at her in the rearview mirror. "Did either of you learn anything interesting about the Chalmers while we were there?"

Kensy nodded. "Tinsley is lovely and I can't imagine that she would ever want to do anything to harm her children – even though I would."

"You just don't like the fact that Van has a massive crush on you," Max said, ducking away from Kensy's attempt to jab him in the ribs.

"I'd like to crush him," Kensy said. She realized she'd forgot to mention the farm manager, Nick, and went on to detail her walk with Tinsley. "He was unloading a whole lot of boxes, but since when do you need formaldehyde on a farm? Don't they use that to preserve dead things?"

"It has many purposes," Fitz said, "but you might want to look it up."

"There were other things too. Aluminum salts and thim-something," she said. The name was on the tip of her tongue, but she couldn't quite catch it. "Why can't I have your photographic memory, Max?"

"You know, Dash lied about what he was doing today," Max said. "We heard him on the phone last night saying something about biohazard transport boxes and a pickup at nine o'clock. He said that if they wanted to play hardball then clearly they had no idea who they were dealing with. And why would they have biohazard boxes at the farm? That's weird too."

"Mmm," Fitz said. "Given that The Chalmers Corporation HQ is in the city and their Australian factory is located out at Norwest, that does seem strange. Dash certainly hasn't lost any of his famous Chalmers charm

— he had half the mothers at the cricket match swooning all over him yesterday and he was loving every second of it. Did Tinsley mention anything about his assistant, Lucy, being at the match?"

"No," Kensy said. "Was she there?"

Fitz nodded. "He hopped into the car with her for a little while and they were talking, but unfortunately I was busy attending to a batsman with a nosebleed, so I couldn't really tell what they were up to."

Fitz drove into the garage and shut off the engine. Kensy had done a quick scout for Curtis, but this time he was nowhere to be seen. The threesome piled out of the car and grabbed their bags.

"I think Song's been busy," Max said as he pushed open the door into the house. A mournful country tune filled the air along with the smell of a freshly baked chocolate cake. The butler was singing at the top of his lungs and hadn't seemed to notice their arrival.

Kensy charged up the stairs into the kitchen, where Song was busy putting the finishing touches to the icing. At the sound of her footsteps, he spun around and threw the spatula at her. Kensy caught it without missing a beat and licked it from top to bottom. "Mmm, my favorite."

"Good afternoon, Miss Kensington. I'm glad you like it." Song turned back to toss sprinkles on top of the cake. "How was your sojourn in the countryside?"

"Strange," the girl said, collapsing onto a stool at the island. "What about you?"

"I called around to the Chalmers' residence and had a lovely cup of tea with Rosa. Her adoration of Mr. Chalmers is quite unnerving, but the woman can certainly make a mean vanilla cake," Song said. He dusted his hands, then turned back to Kensy as Fitz walked into the room to put on the kettle. "She informed me that Dash and Tinsley's marriage is a very happy one and that Mr. Chalmers is the best husband in the world."

"Yeah right," Kensy scoffed. "There's something odd about the whole situation, if you ask me. Cherry Tree Farm is absolutely gorgeous. And there are literally hundreds of photographs of Dash and Tinsley and the children smiling everywhere – in silver frames on sofa tables, on the walls, even in the bathrooms."

Max appeared, having taken his bag straight upstairs. "It made me feel a bit sad about never having had that," he said, sitting down beside his sister. "I suppose it would have been tricky to cart around loads of pictures when we were moving every six months."

Fitz glanced up from where he was pouring boiling water into the teapot. "I'm sorry, Max, I never knew you felt that way."

Kensy scrunched up her nose. "Why would you feel sad? It was totally creepy," she said. "It's like they have this veneer of perfection, but scratch the surface and there's something very weird about that family. Which reminds me – why did they have a photo in their house of Uncle Rupert and a beautiful woman looking as if they're madly in love?"

Song and Fitz exchanged a meaningful look. Fitz poured himself a cup of tea and stirred in a splash of milk. "I suppose you'll probably find out one day, so it might as well be now," he said, and took a long sip of his tea. "Your uncle was engaged to Dash Chalmers' sister, Abigail. She was the love of Rupert's life, but she drowned in an accident before they were married. He never talks about it and you're not to bring it up either – with anyone, including your grandmother."

"That's awful. Poor Uncle Rupert," Kensy said.

"Wow, that's horrible," Max said, frowning. "I'm glad the Chalmers have a photograph of them – there's nothing more important than family. When Mum and Dad come back, I don't care wherever we live, I just know I want there to be pictures."

CHAPTER 32

GZMGIFNH ZMW RMGVIILTZGRLMH

Mr. Thacker sighed loudly. "No," he said, shaking his head. "No, no, no, no, NO! We are not leaving this auditorium until it's perfect, do you hear me?"

Lucienne whimpered and began to cry in the front row.

"Oh goodness," the headmaster said, passing the girl a tissue. "I wasn't talking to you, my dear. I meant the other children." He stepped back to address the rest of the choir. "Surely you all understand that the competition is this Saturday!" he boomed. Little flecks of spit pooled in the corners of his mouth. "And where is Dugald?"

"He went to the bathroom ages ago, sir," Max piped up.

"Well, go and find him then," the man ordered. "And he'd better not be sick or there will be trouble!"

Max didn't relish the idea of dragging the lad out of the bathroom, but he knew better than to argue with the headmaster. The man was seriously obsessed. He'd even had all the sports canceled, with the Wentworth Grammar teams forfeiting their matches just so there was no chance of anyone sneaking off to sports instead of showing up for the concert.

Max pushed open the door to the boys' bathroom and heard whispering. He looked along the row of stalls, which were empty but for one pair of thick ankles.

"I hate it here," Dugald sniveled. "You never said he'd be so mean."

Max felt sorry for the lad. On top of being new to the school, Dugald must be buckling under the pressure of carrying the main male solo. Max turned to step outside to give the lad some privacy.

"Tell my parents I want out. It's not worth it, no matter how good the pay is," the lad said.

Max paused. If Dugald wasn't talking to his parents, who was he speaking to and what was all that about getting paid? Max's hopes of hearing anything more were dashed when two lads barreled in, chatting loudly. He quickly entered the stall beside Dugald's, but the boy whispered a hurried goodbye and hung up. Max waited until he heard the toilet flush then he did the same and walked out to wash his hands.

"You okay?" he asked. "Mr. Thacker sent me to look for you."

Dugald groaned. "Of course he did," he said, patting water on his red face and slicking back his dark hair. "Tell him I've gone home sick."

Max frowned. "Are you?"

"What?"

"Sick?" Max said.

"Of *him*, yes," the boy snapped.

* * *

Choir practice finally finished at half past one, which left the children with ten minutes to eat lunch before their afternoon lessons commenced. Max had managed to cajole Dugald into returning to the rehearsal, though it was obvious from all the huffing and snorting that the boy wasn't happy about it. Between Dugald and Lucienne, Mr. Thacker had laid on the charm thicker than the mortar on a bricklayer's trowel.

"Hey," Max said, tapping his sister on the shoulder, "there's something weird going on with Dugald."

Kensy looked at him quizzically with her mouth full of ham-and-cheese sandwich. There was already a dollop of mayonnaise on her shirt.

Curtis leaned over. "What are you two talking about?" he asked.

Max didn't think it would hurt to include their friend, the amateur sleuth, in the conversation. He and Kensy liked Curtis a lot and the boy was smart too, so he quickly explained what he'd heard in the bathroom.

"We should go and talk to him," Curtis suggested. "You know, I was thinking it was strange that I've never seen him perform with other schools in the choral competition and, come to think of it, I've never seen Lucienne either. It's as if they were both conjured from a land far away."

"That doesn't prove anything," Max said. "They might have gone to schools that didn't enter the competition."

Curtis's face dropped. "It was just an idea."

Kensy looked at her brother, a wry smile perched on her lips. "Okay, Sherlock Holmes, why don't we see what we can find out?"

Curtis's chest puffed up and there was a twinkle in his eye. "I'd recommend that you let me ask the questions. I know what I'm doing."

The twins grinned.

"Clearly," Max said. "Come on, you'd better have your rapid-fire interrogation tactics ready – the bell's due to ring in two minutes."

CHAPTER 33

Z OVZW

Kensy was upstairs in her room, working on an assignment on the history of Taronga Zoo, when Max charged through from their adjoining bathroom. She put down her pen and stretched. They'd been training with ninja stars earlier and her hands had been cramping on and off all afternoon. It hadn't been an entirely successful session, either, with Song making a note to replace two cushions and repair the painting of the harbor bridge in the front room.

"It's them," Max said, snatching a piece of paper and pen from his sister's desk. He spotted her watch on the dressing table and rolled his eyes.

Max quickly took down the message and Kensy checked it. At least her Morse code skills had improved over the past few months, even if her watch-wearing habit was still as questionable as ever.

"What does it say?" Kensy asked.

Max quickly transcribed the message and stood back.

Send Fitz Friday. QT Dalefield S.I. Love, Mum and Dad.

"Well, that's not going to happen," Kensy said. She grabbed a duffel bag and began shoveling the clothes scattered on her bedroom floor into it. "We're only a few hours away from 'SI.' I assume they're on the South Island, and isn't Dalefield near Queenstown? There's nothing there except farms and big beautiful houses. Anyway, we can all go. It's Wednesday, so, if we leave now, we can get there early and surprise Mum and Dad because they still think we're in London." She stopped and grinned at her brother. "Max, we're going to see Mum and Dad! Can you believe it?"

For one glorious moment, Max allowed himself to be carried away by the juggernaut of his sister's flight of fancy. Then reality set in. "That would be amazing," he said gently, "but we should talk to Fitz first. We can't all just abandon the mission."

"Ugh, why do you have to be such a party pooper?" Kensy fell back on her bed with an exasperated sigh.

The front doorbell rang and Song called out to the children. "Your friend from next door is here, and he is insisting that he speak to you both right away."

Kensy sat up on her elbows. "I wonder what mind-blowing discovery he's made now."

"We're coming," Max called back. He left the note on Kensy's desk and headed downstairs with his sister dragging her heels behind him. They found the boy examining the intercom screen in the front foyer.

"Oh, hi," Curtis said, straightening. "I'm so glad you're home. I *really* need to talk to you – it's important."

"I'm sure it is," Kensy said sarcastically, earning herself a glare from her brother.

"Don't be so mean," Max mouthed.

Kensy blushed, wishing she could take back what she'd just said. She liked Curtis and the poor kid suffered enough at the hands of Ellery Chalmers without her being nasty too. She had no right to take her frustrations out on him.

"Let's get a drink," Max said to Curtis. He led the boy up the short flight of stairs and past the kitchen, spotting a stray ninja star poking out of the wall behind the couch in the family room. How it had made its way from the front room was cause for concern. Max motioned for Curtis to sit down facing the other way, then pointed out the weapon to Kensy, who quickly dislodged it and tucked it under a cushion.

Curtis planted himself on the chair and leaned in. "I saw him," he whispered excitedly, his eyes wide.

Song set down three glasses of ice water and a bowl of sweets on the coffee table in front of the children. "I'll be in the laundry if you need me," he said.

Kensy tore open a Violet Crumble and took a bite. "Curtis, you're going to have to be more specific. Who did you see?"

"The man from the ferry whose photos you stole then erased," Curtis said, as if it were the most obvious thing in the world.

Kensy had completely forgotten about the man and hadn't even taken a proper look at the pictures she'd transferred to her phone. "Hey, it wasn't just me," she pointed out. "You helped too."

Curtis grinned. "I suppose I did. So if the police come for us, I promise I won't let you take the fall on your own."

"Where was he?" Max asked.

Curtis took a deep breath. "He drove past in a silver Mazda hatchback – it had a few dents, so he mustn't be a very good driver. He was heading toward the Chalmers' place. Don't worry, I got the license plate." The boy stopped and frowned. "But I don't know any police officers, so it might be hard to run them against a database and I don't think it would be a good idea to go up to North Sydney Police Station and just ask – they might be suspicious or maybe he's already reported us for what we did."

"I'll get my phone," Kensy said, and bounded away upstairs. When she returned, she and Max sat on either side of the boy as she flicked through the pictures. There were some new photos Kensy had taken on the weekend, but once she got past them, she found the others she'd transferred. There was a photo of Ellery and another of Van and then several of the two of them together walking along the street and on the wharf, as well as a few of Dash leaving the family home in his car.

Kensy swiped back to the next image. It was of a white van and a property gate that looked oddly familiar. She studied it closely then realized what it was. "That's Cherry Tree Farm!" she gasped.

"You probably took it on the weekend," Max said.

Kensy shook her head. "No, it's from that man's phone, and don't you think I'd remember if there was a white van going in ahead of us? We were the only ones there. Why does this man have a picture of the Chalmers' farm?"

That was enough to grab Max's attention. "Are there more photos?" he asked, leaning in.

Kensy flicked back to another frame. "That's the shed we saw when Tinsley and I were out walking. The one that Nick said had farm equipment in it, but Mr. Chalmers told us it didn't belong to them. He claimed it was on the property owned by someone whose name I can't recall."

"Davidson," Max said.

Kensy rolled her eyes. "Your freakish abilities never cease to amaze me."

Curtis sat between the twins, turning his head from side to side as if he were watching a vigorous game of tennis. "Okay, you lost me at the gate," he said. "What are you two talking about?"

Kensy and Max explained what they'd gathered so far about the Chalmers' farm and the shed.

Curtis's brow furrowed. "So this man who's been taking pictures of the kids actually *knows* them?"

"Van and Ellery didn't seem to recognize him on the ferry the other day," Max said.

The doorbell buzzed. Song walked through from the laundry and glanced at the screen in the kitchen. A blonde woman with a broad smile was standing outside. He pressed the button to answer. "Hello," he said cheerfully.

"Hello there, it's Mrs. Pepper from next door. I was just wondering if Curtis was with you?" she asked.

Curtis groaned and put his head in his hands. "Seriously, Mum, it couldn't wait?"

"Ah yes, Mrs. Pepper, he is. Would you like to come in?" Song asked.

"Not right now, thank you. I'm a wee bit busy. I'm in the middle of letting down the hems on Curtis's dress pants for the concert on Saturday. He's grown so much lately I need to take *another* measurement before I can finish them. Could you send him home, please?"

"Certainly," said Song.

Kensy twisted her lips to stop from laughing. Max glanced at his sister and chuckled, but managed to pass it off as a cough.

Curtis stood up. "This is really weird and we've still got to get to the bottom of what's going on with Dugald as well. I didn't buy that story about his dad getting a job transfer to Sydney when we talked to him this afternoon."

It seemed that the mysteries were piling up at the moment.

"Bye, Song," Curtis said to the man, who had just turned the leg of lamb that was roasting in the oven.

"Goodbye, Curtis," Song replied.

"Your dinner smells delicious," the boy said with a smile. "And Mum and Dad loved that zucchini bread you made on the weekend."

"Thank you. We must have you and your parents over for a meal soon," the man replied.

"Oh, and thanks for taking me and Mum on a tour the other day. That room downstairs is awesome," Curtis said. "Mum loves the wallpaper – she wanted me to find out where it came from."

As Max walked Curtis to the front door, Kensy looked at the butler with upturned palms. Song smiled and began to peel some potatoes that were sitting beside the sink. Shortly after the front door closed, Max skidded into the kitchen.

"What was that about?" he demanded. "What room downstairs?"

Kensy scurried over to the island. "And since when did you two become best buddies?"

Song looked at the twins innocently. "Curtis is a very sweet and curious boy," he said, pulling a bag of fresh beans from the crisper in the fridge. "He and his mother came for tea and I simply showed them about. He was talking about the cinema room, if you must know."

"But that's on the top floor, where the terrace is," Kensy said with a frown. "Not downstairs."

"Perhaps there is another one," Song said.

Kensy snorted. "That's ridiculous. No house needs two cinema rooms."

Song walked over to the small control pad on the kitchen wall and pressed a button.

The twins almost jumped out of their skins when the coffee table in the family room slid back and a spiral staircase rose up in the middle of the floor.

"Whoa! How come we've never seen this before?" Kensy hurried over and clutched the railing. She and Max ran down into the secret space. "It's not a cinema room," Kensy called as she reached the bottom. "There's nothing in here."

"Oh, forgive me," Song said. He pressed another button, and out of the walls came a bank of seating while a screen dropped from the ceiling. There was even a popcorn machine too.

"This is insane," Max yelled. "I still don't believe it's a cinema room, though."

Song smirked. He pushed yet another button and the furniture disappeared, replaced by four single beds and various other household items.

"Is this a panic room?" Kensy shouted. She was beginning to feel a little panicky herself. She bounded back upstairs with Max hot on her heels. Song pressed another button and the family room returned to normal.

"Why on earth did you show that to Curtis?" Max asked. "I gather it's where we're meant to go if we ever encounter any serious danger while we're here?"

"I had to," Song replied, filling a saucepan with water. "Curtis was very observant during the remodeling. Despite the builder's screens along the boundary, he managed to take many pictures from his back garden. He even drew his own architectural diagrams and, I must say, they were disconcertingly accurate. I tried to convince him it was the hole for the pool, but he showed me his photographs and you could clearly see both. It is fortunate that your grandmother had the room fitted out for myriad uses. That boy has some impressive skills."

"What else haven't we seen?" Kensy asked, climbing onto a stool at the island.

"Perhaps there is a little more, but I thought you two had some investigating to do," Song said.

Max stood beside his sister and nodded.

"First things first. We need to find out who that car is registered to and then we'll see if the Davidsons own the property where the shed is."

Kensy looked at Song. "Could you hack the police database for us?"

The butler had just pulled the lamb out of the oven and was adding the potatoes to the pan. "I would be pleased to," he replied, "however, my computer is updating from the company mainframe and will be for some time yet."

"That's all right. We can do it," Kensy said. She nudged her brother and motioned for them to go upstairs. "Oh well, I better get back to my assignment."

"Me too," Max said, and the two of them scampered up the staircase and into Kensy's room. Max closed the bedroom door. "Unless you've had some lessons I haven't, I don't believe we've covered that part about hacking police databases in the spy curriculum just yet."

"Nope, but Autumn has," Kensy said triumphantly. She fetched her laptop from the end of her bed and opened the lid. "We can catch her before she heads to school."

"Um, no, we can't. What are you going to tell her? Autumn thinks we're in the hospital, or recovering at Alexandria by now," Max reminded her.

"About that," Kensy said sheepishly, "I might have accidentally told Autumn something different. It's not like I meant to – she sort of guessed. Anyway, she doesn't know the details, just that we're on a mission. And she's my best friend, Max. Autumn can keep a secret."

"Fine," Max sighed, eyeballing his sister, "but if Granny finds out, you do know we'll never be trusted again."

Kensy had already begun to place a call to Autumn. Max elbowed her out of the way when the girl appeared on the screen looking a little flustered.

"Max? Oh, I've been so worried," she said as she tied a red ribbon around her braid. "Are you all right?"

"Hi," he said, waving. "I'm in one piece."

"I'm here too." Kensy poked her head into

view. "And I'm great. Thanks for asking – *again*."

Autumn blushed. She stuffed half a dozen bobby pins in her mouth before beginning to fix them in her hair. "What's up?" she mumbled.

"We need your help. Can you run a NSW license plate for us and access the computer at the land titles office in Sydney?" Max asked.

Autumn nodded and quickly finished pinning her hair. "Uh, I think so," she said. "It might take me a little bit of time. When do you need it?"

"Tomorrow morning is fine," Max said.

"Sooner, if you can manage it," Kensy jumped in. She was hoping to leave for New Zealand at the crack of dawn. "I'll stay up until you call back."

Max read out the license plate Curtis had jotted down and passed along the location of the farm as well as the name Davidson.

"How's it all going over there?" Autumn asked. "You've actually been missing some really nice weather for a change. Although, now I've said that, it'll probably start raining."

"It's good," Max said. "Hot. I learned to play cricket and I'm not too bad at it."

Kensy elbowed him out of the way. "He's a superstar and everyone loves him – he's already helped the top team win two matches. I, on the other hand, joined a dance class, which I don't care for at all. I'm not too keen on some of the kids either."

"She means Van," Max teased, shoving Kensy back. "He's totally in love with her. It's fun to watch."

Autumn raised an eyebrow. "You must tell me more, Master Maxim."

"No, he doesn't need to say anything," Kensy said, covering her brother's mouth with one hand. "I'll tell you myself. Van drives me nuts. He's *so* good-looking and *so* popular and *so* full of his own importance. Honestly, I don't know how anyone our age could have a crush on someone – what a waste of energy!" Kensy peered at the screen. "Have you got a fever or something? You look like you're burning up."

Autumn shook her head. "I'm fine."

"Oh, I see," Kensy said, grinning. "Sorry, I'm sure that some pre-teen crushes are absolutely wonderful, just like sunshine, lollipops and rainbows."

Autumn glared at the screen, trying to send Kensy a message. Unfortunately, Max caught it too.

"Kensy's right," Max said, his voice full of concern. "You look like you've got a pain in your stomach or something."

"Um, I'd better go," Autumn said, tugging at the collar of her uniform. "I'll run all of this when I get to school. I've got a lesson downstairs first thing, so I can access the mainframe. I'll call you as soon as I can."

"Thanks, Autumn, you're the best," Max said, flashing her a smile.

Even from over 10,000 miles away, and via a video link, Kensy didn't miss her friend go weak at the knees. "Seriously, Autumn," she said, laughing, "I can still see you."

And with that the girl disappeared from the screen.

CHAPTER 34

Z XOFV

Kensy and Max were upstairs when they heard Fitz arrive home. After their chat to Autumn, Kensy had gone to her room to finish off some urgent math homework while Max lay on his bed, reading. Although neither of them were thinking much about what they were doing – their minds, instead, were fixated on the fact that a reunion with their parents was imminent.

Fitz headed straight upstairs and was confronted by the twins at the top of the landing. The looks on their faces said it all.

"We were right that Mum and Dad are in New Zealand, and they've asked for you to go. You need to be there on Friday," Kensy blurted.

Max passed him the decoded message. Fitz looked at it, then nodded his head, giving nothing away.

"But we're coming with you and we should go tomorrow," Kensy said. "They don't know how close we are."

"And they're not going to," Fitz said without a shred of emotion. He'd just come from the longest staff meeting in history and was quite literally itching to have a shower and relax after what had been a very tough day.

Kensy frowned. "What do you mean?"

"I'm not going against their instructions," Fitz said.

Max's stomach twisted. He knew Fitz was right, but it didn't stop him from feeling a pang of disappointment.

"But we're still coming, right?" Kensy said. She looked from Fitz to Max, then back to Fitz.

The man shook his head. "You'll stay here with Song. I'm not putting the two of you in harm's way. We have no idea what to expect and this is best left to the professionals."

"What!" Kensy exploded. "That's ridiculous! We saved the prime minister's son in Italy and brought down the Diavolo – we're professional too, you know!"

Max put a hand on his sister's arm, but she shook it off.

"Don't touch me!" Kensy yelled. "Why are you on his side, anyway? What's wrong with you, Max? Don't you want to be with Mum and Dad?"

"Of course I do, but think about it, Kens – they've made plans for a reason and they didn't ask for us to be involved. I want them back as much as you do," Max said. He couldn't help but be hurt by such an accusation.

"No, you don't!" Kensy spat. Before anyone could stop her, she flew downstairs and out the front door.

Max started to chase after her, but Fitz placed a heavy hand on his shoulder. "Leave her be," he said. "She'll only be able to listen once she's calmed down."

Max knew that was true. There was no point trying to talk to Kensy when she was this worked up. A run around the block would do her the world of good. Maybe then they could have a rational discussion. Or maybe they wouldn't talk about it at all.

"She's wrong," Max said. He could feel his eyes prickling. "I miss them every bit as much as she does. I hate it when she says things like that because it's just not true."

"I know you do, mate," Fitz said, and wrapped his muscly arms around the lad. Max leaned against the man's chest, completely overcome. This time he allowed himself to cry until there were simply no tears left.

* * *

"Should we go and look for her?" Max said, glancing at the kitchen clock for the hundredth time. The ticking was beginning to drive him crazy. It was just after seven and Kensy still wasn't home. "She might've gotten lost." He didn't like to think that anything else could have happened to her.

"That is a very good point, Master Maxim," Song said. "Your sister has not been blessed with your navigational skills." The butler had already wiped a dozen imaginary spots off the counter and cleaned the sink twice.

Fitz looked up from where he was sitting on the couch, reading the day's issue of the *Beacon*. Although Max noticed he hadn't turned a page in over twenty minutes. "I'm sure she'll be back soon, especially when she remembers she'll be missing one of Song's famous baked dinners."

But the tone in the man's voice betrayed his concerns too. Song started serving up as Max hopped down from the island and the front door flew open.

"I saw him!" Kensy exclaimed as she tore upstairs to the kitchen. "In the window of an apartment in that high-rise just down from the Chalmers' place. He has a telescope and it was trained on their house. And I'm pretty sure the woman who was at the house the night Mrs. Chalmers disappeared was there too – Lucy, Dash's assistant. What's that about?"

Max frowned. "I wonder if Autumn has managed to run those plates yet or find out about the land."

Fitz and Song cast the children quizzical looks. "What are you talking about?" Fitz asked. "You haven't told Autumn where we are, have you?"

"It was an accident and, besides, she's not going to tell anyone. Song's computer was busy – we had to get on it," Kensy said, then regaled Fitz and Song with the story of the man from the ferry and what they'd realized about the photos Kensy had stolen from him. It seemed she'd forgotten all about her earlier outburst and, while Fitz was not impressed about her speaking to her friend, there was nothing he could do about it now except to ensure Cordelia didn't find out.

"Don't you think it's weird that we're supposed to be protecting the children from Mrs. Chalmers and yet there's this man who's watching them and taking pictures and he's been at the farm too?" Kensy said.

"Maybe he works for Dash," Max said.

"There's something fishy about him, that's for sure." Kensy yawned and stretched. "I'm starving. I've been watching the unit for ages." She grabbed two of the dinner plates from the island and placed them on the table. Song brought over the other two.

"Are you okay, Kensy?" Fitz asked as he took his seat.

"Well, if you mean am I happy about you going to New Zealand without us, the answer is no. But I remembered something Mr. Reffell said in one of our strategy lessons the other week, so if you have to go alone then fine. Just make sure you come back and bring Mum and Dad with you," the girl said, stabbing her fork into a crispy baked potato.

Max took a bite of lamb and smiled at his sister.

"Anyway, we're going to be busy on the weekend winning the Choral Competition at the Opera House. Sorry, Song, you have to come and watch now that Fitz has better things to do," Kensy said.

"It would be my pleasure, Miss Kensington and Master Maxim. I do hope there are some country tunes in the repertoire," Song said.

Max grinned. "Not this time, but hopefully you'll still enjoy it. Our choir sounds pretty good considering we've only had a couple of weeks to learn the song."

"Yes, but we've been rehearsing about four hours each day," Kensy grumbled. A worrying thought entered her mind. "Are you going to tell Granny about Autumn?" she asked timidly.

Fitz shook his head. "Not this time. There's no point upsetting her, but please don't make a habit of divulging information when you've specifically been told not to."

"Oh dear," Song said, flushing, "I had meant to tell you all that Dame Spencer called earlier to see how everyone was. I told her you'd had a good weekend in the countryside, and she said that the house is already starting to take shape and she may finally have a lead."

The twins looked at each other.

"I wonder what it is," Max said, cutting a tender piece of lamb and loading it onto his fork with some gravy and beans.

"She did not say," Song said apologetically.

Dinner was a far happier affair than anyone had anticipated. By the time the children polished off Song's chocolate pudding and ice cream, no one would ever have guessed about the earlier blowup. The twins bid Fitz and Song good night, then hurried upstairs to Max's room to check in with Autumn and found they'd already missed a call from her. Max quickly tried to connect.

"Hi there," Autumn said. The twins were both on the screen and gave her a wave.

"Where are you?" Max asked, trying to make out what was in the background.

"Downstairs in the secure room. I was just about to give up – I've got English and Witherbee is on the warpath about students being late to class."

"Sorry, we won't keep you," the boy said.

"What have you found out?" Kensy asked.

Autumn looked down at some notes she had made and read out her findings. "The car is registered to a George Kapalos. The property is owned by a company called Dalefield and the trustee is The Chalmers Corporation. The Davidson family sold it two years ago," Autumn said, looking pleased with herself. She glanced at her watch and grimaced. "Sorry, I've got to go, but call me tomorrow, okay?"

"Thanks, Autumn," Max said, flashing her a grin. "I could kiss you right now."

Autumn's eyes bulged. With her cheeks burning, the girl fumbled around to end the call.

"Yeah, thanks," Kensy said as the screen went black. She stared at it, her mind racing a million miles per second, until Max voiced what was on both of their minds.

"Why would Dash Chalmers have lied to his wife about owning that land?" he said.

"Exactly." Kensy slumped back onto the boy's bed. She lay there for a moment then sat bolt upright. "Dalefield – that's the name in Mum and Dad's message. You don't think it's connected, do you?"

"I mean, it's a stretch. There are probably a million things called Dalefield." Max typed the word into the computer, bringing up over 88,000 results.

"Well, we know Dash Chalmers is hiding something," Kensy said. "And George Kapalos might just hold the key to his secrets. Come on, let's see what we can find out about him."

CHAPTER 35

GSV OLMTVHG WZB

Max had hardly slept at all when he heard the door to his room creak open and Fitz's face appear.

"Sorry, mate, I didn't mean to wake you," the man said.

"I wasn't asleep."

Fitz walked further into the room and sat on the edge of the boy's bed.

Thursday had been much the same as every other school day so far with hours of choir practice followed by cricket training and enough homework to last a week. He and Kensy had made some progress with their investigations into George Kapalos. The man was a freelance journalist and the fact that he was meeting with Dash's assistant, Lucy, probably meant that he was writing a story on Dash and the company. Given there had been a recent announcement that The Chalmers Corporation was now the richest pharmaceutical company in the world, it seemed feasible. Unfortunately, there had been no headway with Dugald or Dash. At least today there was a strong likelihood Fitz would see their parents and, with any luck, they'd all be reunited soon – and maybe with their mother's parents too.

"I'll be back before you know it," Fitz said, giving Max a hug. "And for goodness' sake, make sure you win that choir competition. Thacker's been in a worse mood than usual." The man stood up and walked out of the room. He'd already been in to kiss Kensy goodbye. She hadn't even stirred.

Max hopped out of bed and walked to the door. He pulled it open. "Good luck," he whispered loudly.

Fitz turned and gave him a nod before disappearing downstairs.

*   *   *

Friday felt like it would never end. The headmaster had timetabled an all-day rehearsal, which had gone from the heights of perfection to the depths of despair – and that was just Thacker himself. The man had more mood swings than the average domestic cat. Thankfully, Dugald hadn't made good on his threat to leave, but Mr. Thacker spent a lot of time cajoling the lad and telling him how amazing he was. He did the same with Lucienne. The pair of them didn't seem to be getting on terribly well either, although that hadn't affected their singing – it was just the arguing during the breaks that was a little uncouth. Kensy hoped they'd be able to control themselves on stage at the Opera House. While she hadn't been especially keen on the choir in the first place, now that they'd come this far, she was rather hoping they'd win.

Just when everyone was certain rehearsal was over, Mr. Thacker announced they were all off to wardrobe to have their outfits double-checked by Ms. Skidmore. Kensy couldn't understand why they weren't able to wear their school uniforms, especially as the concert was scheduled for midday. While Max had tried on at least a dozen tuxes when they'd gone shopping – which Kensy thought ridiculous, given they were practically identical – it had taken her all of two minutes to select an outfit: a long dark-pink skirt with a lighter pink top – not a color combination she would have necessarily gone for, but it was the first thing the shop assistant showed her and it fit, so it would do. Song had insisted Kensy purchase new shoes as well, but she wasn't to be persuaded. She was going to wear her favorite boots whether Ms. Skidmore approved or not. Max thought the outfit looked great, but knew that was best kept to himself, unlike Van, who complimented Kensy loudly in front of everyone, earning himself a terrifying death stare from the girl.

There was no news from Fitz or their parents, which was to be expected, as Fitz would only have arrived in New Zealand mid-afternoon. Although it was a short flight from Sydney to Queenstown, there was a two-hour jump ahead in time zones. Kensy and Max had decided the best way to keep their minds off what might have been happening was to ramp up their own investigations.

After their outfits were approved, Mr. Thacker decided on a last run-through of the song and another detailed explanation of what was to happen in the morning. They were to meet at the Opera House at eleven sharp, dressed and ready to perform. The competition commenced at midday. He expected them to get no less than nine hours' sleep tonight and eat a hearty breakfast, though nothing too stodgy. It was just after four o'clock when they were finally dismissed.

"Is Song coming to get us?" Kensy asked her brother as they walked from the auditorium, lugging their schoolbags and clothes for the concert.

Max took his phone out of his blazer pocket and looked at the screen. "He's in the parking lot and he says that we're taking Ellery and Van as well." Max turned and called out to Van that they were all going together.

"How are you getting home, Curtis?" Kensy asked the boy, who was walking along beside her, his suit bag dragging on the ground.

"Ferry," he said.

"Don't be ridiculous – you can come with us," the girl said, earning herself a grin from Max and a sneer from Ellery.

Song was standing beside the car dressed in a pair of white trousers, a royal-blue polo shirt with brown boat shoes and some very stylish new sunglasses.

"Looking sharp, Song," Kensy said, waggling her eyebrows. "New outfit?"

Song grinned. "I thought I would treat myself."

"Where's Mum?" Ellery asked anxiously as they reached the man.

"Your mother had an appointment that was

running late," the butler replied, and added, "She's fine, I assure you." He didn't want the child to worry that something else untoward could have happened to the woman.

"Where's your dad?" Van said, realizing that Fitz wasn't with them. He opened the door for Kensy and motioned for her to go ahead.

"He's on a course," Max said at the same moment Kensy claimed the man had taken ill. They looked at each other.

"Gerry had been at a course all day but has come down with a dreadful flu," Song explained. "I have been making chicken soup by the pot load."

"Yuck, I hate chicken soup," Ellery said. She tugged open the car door and climbed into the back seat.

Max and Curtis forged through to the very back while Kensy hopped in beside Ellery. Van took the front seat, although not without looking a little disappointed.

Song buckled his seat belt and put the keys in the ignition. "Does everyone have everything they need?" he asked.

"No!" Curtis gasped. "Sorry, I've left my dress shoes in the dressing room. I need them for the concert." He pushed the chair in front of him forward, almost catapulting Ellery into the back of Song's seat.

"Hey! Watch it, Pepper!" she grouched.

"I'll come with you," Kensy offered, keen to put some space between herself and the girl.

She and Curtis scrambled out of the car and sprinted back through the playground. The doors to the building were still open, but there was no one about. Curtis rushed into the dressing room while Kensy waited in the foyer. He returned in no time, triumphantly holding up a black shoe bag as if it were a trophy. They were about to leave when they heard the headmaster's voice coming from inside the auditorium and he didn't sound happy.

"Let's see what's going on," Curtis said. "We can get to the stage from here."

Kensy couldn't resist, and the pair hurried through the building and down a long passageway. Curtis pushed open a door and they tiptoed backstage, where he and Kensy peered through a gap in the black curtains. Mr. Thacker and a haughty-looking woman wearing a teal suit were in the middle of a heated exchange.

"We had a deal, Susan," Mr. Thacker boomed.

"Well, I don't like this deal anymore, *Thaddeus*," the woman retorted. "My client claims you have caused him considerable distress and he no longer wants to participate."

"He can't do that! We need him," the man hissed through gritted teeth.

Kensy and Curtis looked at one another.

"Take it or leave it – either you deposit another ten thousand into the account by tonight or I'm afraid that my client will no longer be involved."

Thaddeus Thacker opened his mouth to speak, but the woman pressed a black talon against his lips. "There will be no further discussion and no more hissy fits. It's unbecoming for a man of your stature. Just pay the money and everything will work out exactly the way you want," she said, then turned on her spiky black heels and stalked up the aisle toward the exit.

Mr. Thacker rested his head in his hands and began to cry, which Kensy thought was even more unbecoming for a man in his position. It was so awful that she and Curtis decided it was time to go too, which was just as well because the cleaners turned out the lights two minutes later.

"What was all that about?" Curtis asked as they ran for the car.

"I wonder who her client is," Kensy said.

"There she is!" Curtis pointed to the other side of the parking lot, where the woman was stepping into a black sports car. Beside her was a man and in the back seat was none other than Dugald McCrae.

"Whoa! Do you think Mr. Thacker's been paying that kid to be in the choir?" Curtis asked.

"I mean, he would have to be insane," Kensy said, "but it sure seems like it. We need hard evidence – more than just overhearing a conversation."

As they approached their car, Van leapt out to open the door for Kensy. Curtis clambered in first, accidentally whacking Ellery with his shoe bag as he made his way to the very back.

"Ow!" she whined, but no one paid her any attention.

For the entire journey home, Kensy stared out the window, wondering about her parents and Fitz and hoping that their mission was going to plan. Curtis was equally preoccupied, mulling over what Kensy had said. He knew Mr. Thacker liked to win, but the idea that the headmaster would pay some kid to be in their choir was madness – wasn't it?

* * *

Tinsley Chalmers had everything she needed. She'd packed three small carry-on bags with a change of clothes and underwear, their pajamas and toiletries. She had money to buy clothes when they arrived at their destination, but in the meantime, they'd just have to make do. The bags were hidden in the bottom of her wardrobe. This time tomorrow they'd be gone.

And now she had a foolproof plan to get Dash out of the picture too. If all went well, she and the children would be on a flight to the other side of the world before he even realized they were missing.

CHAPTER 36

Z KVIULINZMXV GL IVNVNYVI

"Right, we are going out this evening, children," Song announced, once they'd dropped their other passengers home. It hadn't gone unnoticed that, despite Van's best efforts to talk to Kensy, and Ellery whining that she was likely to have a bruise where Curtis had whacked her with his shoe bag, the twins had hardly said a word the whole way home.

"Where?" Max asked flatly. Like his sister, his mind had been on his parents ever since leaving school.

Song grinned. "It is a surprise. We are doing something I never imagined I would, followed by a delicious meal – but we must hurry. You need to change and then we are off!"

"Are you just trying to keep us busy so we don't have time to think about Fitz?" Kensy asked.

Song frowned and shook his head. "I have no idea what Mr. Fitz's current engagement entails."

"Of course you do. I bet you know exactly what's going on," Max said. "I mean, Granny probably trusts you and Sidney more than anyone."

"Confucius says you cannot open a book without learning something," Song replied. "Similarly, you cannot live in this household without knowing a little. But a little knowledge is a dangerous thing, so perhaps it is best to stay in the dark. Please, children, I promise we will have an enjoyable evening and the time will pass much more quickly and then tomorrow we have all the excitement of the concert at the Sydney Opera House, no less."

"If you say so," Kensy sighed, trudging up to her room.

Meanwhile, Curtis pushed a cart down a supermarket aisle, deep in thought. His mother had insisted he help her, but he was dying to get home. He had an idea that he was keen to share with Kensy and Max.

A half hour later, having unpacked the groceries, Curtis asked his mother if he could go next door. With his backpack fully stocked, he stood on the porch at number two and rang the buzzer. He waited an age, but no one came. Curtis took a deep breath. Having Kensy and Max by his side would have been a bonus, but if they weren't available, he'd just have to go it alone.

* * *

"I look ridiculous," Kensy griped as they hurried up the Opera House steps. She tugged at her skirt, wishing she could have worn pants.

"You look great," Max said, adjusting his bow tie. "I mean it."

Kensy shot him a smile. "I feel sorry for you in that suit. You must be so hot and, no, for your information I didn't say you *looked* hot."

"You both look very smart," Song said. "I would like to take a photograph for your grandmother and Mr. Fitz. Let's see if we can manage to get the bridge in the background too."

Last night, the children and Song had climbed the Harbour Bridge at twilight. The view was breathtaking with the western sunset and the sparkling city lights. They then had dinner at one of Song's favorite restaurants, where the dumplings were even better than his — if that was possible. The children had loved every minute and were glad that Song had organized to take them out.

Song snapped a couple of shots before the twins insisted he hop in too and master the art of the selfie. After several misfires, they finally got a picture with all of them in the frame.

Max glanced at his watch. "We better head in before Mr. Thacker has an aneurysm."

The trio entered the foyer, where there

were already hundreds of children and parents milling about. There was an undeniable buzz in the air. Max and Kensy went to join their choir while Song spotted Curtis's parents and walked over to say hello. Van gasped when he saw Kensy.

The girl shook her head vigorously and pointed her finger at him. "Don't you dare say a word," she warned.

Van frowned in confusion and was swiftly whisked out of harm's way by Max.

"Someone's feeling the heat," Kensy said to Curtis, when she noticed the trail of perspiration running down their headmaster's temples. Ms. Skidmore was prancing about, checking that everyone looked perfect.

"And so he should," the boy replied mysteriously. "I know what he's up to."

Kensy looked at the lad. "We *think* we know what he's up to, but we don't have any proof."

"I do," Curtis said with a glint in his eye. But before he could say another word, Miss Sparks declared that all singers needed to assemble backstage. The bells were ringing too, signaling for audience members to take their seats.

Kensy noticed Curtis had his trusty backpack with him, which clashed horribly with his tuxedo. She wondered what he thought he might need for the concert.

"Right," the headmaster hissed, "I don't want to hear one peep out of any of you unless we're warming up or on stage singing. Voice preservation is the name of the game from here on in and, if I see anyone flouting the rules, you will be on playground beautification for the rest of the term."

The children were led through a series of backstage doors and down a labyrinth of tunnels to a large dressing room, where there were several other schools already waiting. The stage manager read the list of performances in order, with Wentworth Grammar scheduled last of all. In total, there were twelve choirs, which was apparently a lot less than previous years due to the competition being brought so far forward.

Kensy and Curtis sat in the corner so they could continue their conversation, hoping that the other children would provide cover, but Mr. Thacker had eyes everywhere. Miss Sparks and Ms. Skidmore were patrolling like commandants. At one point Kensy opened her mouth and was shushed by both of them before she'd uttered a word. Soon enough Mr. Thacker directed the children to another rehearsal space to warm up, where they were *he-he*ing, *ha-ha*ing and *mo-mo*ing with gusto.

Twenty minutes later, the group were called to line up at the side of stage. The twins saw the interior of the vast concert hall for the first time with its soaring geometrical ceiling, odd-looking acoustic treatments that resembled transparent donuts hanging on thin wires, and rows of red seats that seemed to rise into the heavens.

"Wow!" Max gasped, garnering himself a glare from Ms. Skidmore.

The audience was in raptures for the choir that had just performed and the woman at the front was taking an awful lot of bows.

"Thank you, Miss Stephenson and the remarkable Stonehurst Singers!" The emcee grinned widely, revealing a mouthful of gleaming white teeth, as the group filed off to the right and the Wentworth Grammar Choristers entered from stage left.

Thaddeus Thacker assumed his position at the podium while Mrs. Strump took her place at the piano. The children quickly filed onto the risers and Kensy scanned the audience for Song. Curtis nudged her when he spotted the man next to his parents. The Chalmers were in the same row a little further along.

Mr. Thacker raised his hand in the air and the music began. Eight and a half minutes later, with Dugald and Lucienne's voices stealing the show, they were enveloped by resounding applause. Mr. Thacker's grin couldn't have been any wider.

"We have come to the end of the program," the emcee declared. "You may have noticed that all of the choirs are now seated in the boxes on either side of the stage. Wentworth Grammar Choristers, please take the seats directly behind you and, while we await the adjudication, we will be treated to an organ solo of JS Bach's 'Toccata and Fugue in D Minor' from the talented Miss Kitty Warburton."

There was a small groan from the audience as several people were obviously aware of the rather lengthy nature of the piece. The children sat in silence, watching and waiting. Kensy noticed that, despite her stylish appearance in a very pretty floral dress, Tinsley Chalmers looked as if she carried the weight of the world on her shoulders. When Dash reached across for his wife's hand, the woman visibly flinched before taking it. Finally, the emcee walked to the podium to announce the winner. Thaddeus Thacker sat at the end of the row, poised to leap up and accept the prize. His archnemesis, Simone Stephenson, flashed him a strange smile.

"Well, ladies and gentleman, boys and girls, what a stunning competition we have had." The emcee exhaled dramatically. "I can barely believe the result. The stronghold, it seems, has been broken." Thaddeus Thacker took in a sharp breath as Simone Stephenson's smug expression melted from her face. "This year's equal runners-up are the Wentworth Grammar Choristers and the Stonehurst Singers." The man's voice reached a crescendo, which was met with rousing applause.

"We came second – that's pretty good," Max said to Van.

"And now it gives me the greatest of pleasure to announce the winner of the Sydney Choral Competition, on their first attempt, is the Dingley Academy Choir." The emcee clapped enthusiastically. The small group that had performed early on in the program were seated in the furthest corner from the stage. The significance of the win was not lost on them or their young choir master. The man was fist pumping the air while the children were squealing and hugging each other.

Thaddeus Thacker's baton snapped in his hand. "I demand a recount!" he yelled.

"Me too!" Simone Stephenson said, shooting out of her seat.

There was a gasp from the audience.

"That's not exactly the sort of behavior I'd expected to see here," Max whispered to Van, who was doing his best not to laugh.

The emcee chortled nervously and looked into the wings for some indication as to what to do. "Mr. Thacker, Miss Stephenson, please take your seats," he said uncertainly.

Thaddeus stamped his foot like a petulant child. "She stole my best singers by offering them scholarships to Stonehurst," he accused, pointing a finger at Simone Stephenson.

The woman rolled her eyes. "Thaddeus, I didn't *steal* them – I saw an opportunity, that's all, darling."

"Darling?" The word was loudly repeated by half the audience.

To the side of the stage, Divorah Skidmore looked as if she'd swallowed a toad. Had that woman, Thaddeus's sworn enemy, just called him "darling"?

Curtis Pepper couldn't contain himself any longer. He leapt to his feet. "Mr. Thacker paid Dugald McCrae and Lucienne Russo to sing in our choir," he said loudly.

Dugald's plump face turned the color of beets while Lucienne slunk down as far as she could in her seat.

The gasps grew louder.

"You can't say that, we don't have any proof," Kensy said. She tugged on Curtis's trousers to get him to sit down.

"I have evidence," he declared, pulling out a wad of papers from his pants pocket. He held them aloft.

"What's that?" Kensy asked.

"I broke into Mr. Thacker's office and it was all there," the boy replied in hushed tones.

Kensy grinned at the lad. "So, you finally got to use those skeleton keys."

Curtis didn't have the heart to tell her that the cleaner let him in because he said he'd left something he needed for the concert inside.

It wasn't long before the parents began calling foul and demanding that Wentworth Grammar and Stonehurst be disqualified.

"The lad's delirious," Thaddeus declared. He looked over at Simone Stephenson. "Sit down, my love. We'll talk about it at home."

That came as an even bigger shock.

"Are you married or something?" one of the children called out.

"Something like that," Thaddeus said.

"We thought you hated each other," another child yelled.

"I wouldn't go that far," Simone Stephenson replied with a wry grin. "A bit of healthy competition does wonders for a relationship."

That was the final straw for Divorah. She strode out of the wings and onto the stage. "Curtis Pepper is telling the truth," she said, casting the headmaster a look that would have shriveled grapes. "Mr. Thacker paid those two children, both of whom are professional singers and have been working overseas for the past couple of years. Thaddeus cheated and, I am ashamed to say, I helped him." Divorah then turned and fled from the stage as the Dingley Academy Choir reached the emcee.

The man tugged at his bow tie and ran a hand through his shiny black hair. "Well, what an interesting . . . um, interesting, um . . . yes, let's move on, shall we? I believe the judges are going to make another announcement about the runners-up. In the meantime, let's not allow what's just happened to overshadow this glorious moment for the Dingley Academy Choir."

"Wow, Curtis, I can't believe you did that," Max whispered, leaning forward to squeeze the lad's shoulder.

Kensy followed up with a jab to Curtis's arm. "That was so brave," she said proudly. "You're amazing."

Van gazed adoringly at the girl. "Not as amazing as you are, Kensington Grey," he said. Fortunately for him, the first bars of the Dingley Academy encore drowned out his words and Kensy was none the wiser.

CHAPTER 37

LM GSV IRTSG GIZXP

The children burst into the foyer and spotted Song standing with the Chalmers and Peppers.

"That concert was far more exciting than anyone expected," Song said. "Your father will be disappointed to have missed it – poor man is full of the flu." Everyone had been glad to hear he'd stayed away as flu in the height of a Sydney summer was not what anyone wanted.

Curtis's father ruffled the boy's sandy hair and beamed with pride. "I didn't know we had a secret agent in the family. Well done, mate – nothing better than seeing corruption dealt with in a swift and timely manner. I'm intrigued as to how you came by that evidence."

"I hope you all said goodbye to Mr. Thacker because you won't be seeing him anytime soon," Dash said. He'd just heard via one of his contacts on the school council that the movers would have the man's office packed up before he left the Opera House.

Kensy couldn't help noticing that Tinsley Chalmers was still looking anxious. The woman had glanced at her phone at least a half-dozen times, as if she were waiting for an important call. But it was her husband's phone that rang again. This time he took himself out of the group to answer it.

"Are you serious?" Dash said, much louder than he'd intended. Max took a backward step to better hear the conversation. "What do you mean the transporter hasn't arrived? Have you tried Lucy? She always picks up."

At the mention of the woman's name, Tinsley Chalmers stiffened. She looked at her phone again and seemed to be reading a message on the screen.

"Those vaccines need to get out tonight or we'll miss the connections. Right, make sure everything is up from the lab and have the Dalefield gate opened so I can drive straight in."

Max felt as though he'd been punched in the stomach by the heavyweight champion of the world. The words "Dalefield" and "lab" in the same sentence just took on a whole new significance.

"I'll leave in ten minutes, but don't expect to see me for a couple of hours," the man said.

From the expression on her brother's face, Kensy immediately knew that something was up and it was serious.

Dash Chalmers walked back to the group. "Sorry, darling, I've got to go to the farm — there's been a break-in and the police need me to see if there's anything missing."

"I'll come with you, Dad," Van offered.

"No," Tinsley snapped, startling everyone. "I have a surprise for the children this afternoon. What a pity you have to go. I was looking forward to all of us doing something together."

"What is it?" Ellery asked.

"If I told you, it wouldn't be a surprise, sweetheart," Tinsley said, and looked at her watch. She needed to get the children home and changed quick smart. "Can you drop us off on your way?" she asked Dash.

"What? Just get a taxi," the man said. "See you later, kids, and well done – although you are a bunch of losers." Dash chuckled and hurried away.

"We can take you," Song offered.

But Max had other ideas.

He walked over and spoke to the butler quietly. "Can Kensy and I have a look around the shops? We want to get something special for Granny and Mum and Dad." He mouthed the last part of the sentence so no one else could hear.

Song grinned. "I will take Mrs. Chalmers and the children home and you can call me if you want a lift. Although perhaps you are both a bit overdressed for a shopping expedition."

Max shook his head. "That's all right. We might get some extra-special attention."

"What are we doing?" Kensy whispered.

"I'll tell you on the way," her brother said.

"Can't we go home and get changed?" she asked, feeling horribly self-conscious.

Max shook his head. "There's no time."

The Peppers were staying to have lunch at one of the restaurants along the concourse. Curtis gave a reluctant wave as the rest of the group walked to the entrance of the parking lot, which, like the Opera House it serviced, was something of an engineering masterpiece, spiraling into the earth in two directions like a double helix beneath the botanic gardens.

"We'll see you later," Kensy said.

"Why don't you come over for a swim after Mum's surprise?" Van suggested.

"That would be great, thanks," Max said.

But there was no way Kensy was going around there unless it was absolutely necessary. She was stunned when Tinsley Chalmers rushed over and gave her then Max a huge hug.

"Great job, kids – you were all wonderful today," the woman said, glassy-eyed. "Come on, Van, Ellery, we need to get home."

And with that she hurried down the tunnel into the parking lot with Song leading the way.

* * *

As the train pulled into the platform, Kensy glanced at the information board.

"I don't see why we couldn't just steal a car," she whispered. "It'd be much faster than this."

The children hopped on and found a seat at the back of the car, away from the other commuters.

"Are you sure that's what he said?" Kensy asked.

Max nodded. "We have to go – what if Mum and Dad have gotten it wrong and they're right here? Even if *we're* wrong, at least we'll know for sure. You did say that Nick was unloading boxes of chemicals last weekend – there very well could be a lab in that shed."

"Why didn't you tell Song? He could have driven us," Kensy said.

Max was beginning to wonder the same thing, but it was too late now.

The twins sat side by side, deep in thought. The enormity of the situation was almost overwhelming. The train rolled in and out of stations, the clack of the wheels on the tracks a welcome distraction.

"I'm starving, Max," Kensy complained. She could hear her stomach grumbling and wished they'd thought to get something to eat before they'd hopped on the train.

"I'll go and see if there's anything further back," Max said, hoping for a dining car. But when he returned, he brought more than a bag of chips and bottle of water with him.

"Curtis, what are you doing here?" Kensy gasped.

The boy smiled and shrugged.

"You can't be here – you have to get off at the next station and go back to your parents. They'll be worried sick about you," Kensy said.

Curtis's eyes dropped to the floor. "Sorry, I just thought maybe I could help with whatever you're doing because you're clearly not shopping for a present for your grandmother and I thought your mother was dead."

"Your ears really are like radars," Max said.

"No, we're not," Kensy admitted, "and that's why you have to go back."

Curtis sat down opposite them and pulled a sandwich from his backpack, breaking the half in two and passing it to Kensy.

"How did you even get away from your parents? You were all going to have lunch, weren't you?" Kensy asked with her mouth full.

"Yes, but then I saw you two walking ahead of us. I told Mum and Dad you'd invited me to go with you and they said it was fine," Curtis said. "They're so happy we're friends. It's just that, you know, Wentworth Grammar hasn't always been the easiest place to find my tribe and you guys are awesome."

Now Kensy felt mean. Max looked at his sister and tugged at his left ear.

"Okay," Kensy relented, "you can come with us, but you have to do everything we say without question."

The lad crossed his heart with his right hand. "I promise I'll be helpful."

"And if the situation turns dangerous, I want you to get out of the way, okay?" Max said.

Curtis bit his lip and nodded. He had no idea what was going on, but this was fast turning out to be the most exhilarating day of his life.

CHAPTER 38

Z HFIKIRHV ZIIREZO

"What on earth are you doing here?" Rupert Spencer called through the open driver's window.

Song spun around, startled, from where he was picking up the newspaper from the driveway. "Good afternoon, sir. Perhaps I could ask you the same thing."

"I asked first," Rupert said.

Song sighed. He was in no way inclined to play games with the man. "I think we should speak inside," he said, gesturing toward the house. "I will make some tea."

"I don't have time for your dratted tea!" Rupert thundered. When he paused to take a breath, Song noticed how disheveled the man appeared. "Sorry, I just need to find out where Dash Chalmers' farm is. I don't suppose you have any idea?"

Song frowned and wondered if he should tell the man. "May I ask, sir, why you are enquiring?"

"His housekeeper told me that's where he is and I need to speak to him – urgently. He has some serious explaining to do." Rupert flexed his fingers, gripping and releasing the steering wheel.

"It is in the Southern Highlands," Song said after a lengthy pause.

"Right, hop in," Rupert said. "I have a feeling this might take two of us."

"But I must wait for the children," Song protested. "They are shopping in the city."

"Call them," Rupert ordered.

Song dialed Max's phone, but the boy didn't pick up. Neither did Kensy. He then activated the GPS and was stunned to find the twins were somewhere near Mittagong and moving quickly along the railway line. "Mr. Rupert, sir, they are not where I expected them to be," Song said, his mouth set in a grim line. He hurried around to the other side of the car and jumped into the passenger seat. "And I suspect that, for reasons unbeknownst to me, they are heading to the same place as you."

Rupert planted his foot on the accelerator. "You'd better hope we get to Dash before the children, old man, or heaven knows what we might find."

CHAPTER 39

WZOVURVOW

"How far is it from the station to the farm?" Kensy asked. There was a storm coming. She could smell it in the air and there was a bank of dark clouds rolling in from the south.

"A couple of miles," Max said.

Kensy sighed and scrunched up her empty chip packet. "It'll take ages to get there," she griped.

Max looked at the map on his phone. Even though he'd committed it to memory, this time he wanted to be doubly sure. "I have an idea," he said as the train pulled out of

Moss Vale Station. By now they were the only ones left on the train. "Curtis, let's see what equipment you have in that backpack of yours."

There was a Swiss Army knife, his skeleton keys, a length of rope, a water bottle, something that may have been a brownie at some point but was now a squashed lump in plastic wrap, a compass, binoculars and a magnifying glass. Max took the knife and, using the longest blade, pried open the car door.

"What are you doing?" Curtis whispered. He looked around to make sure no one was watching.

"We're getting off," Max replied.

Kensy wrinkled her nose. "Are you serious?"

Curtis's jaw fell open, horrified at the thought. "But the train's moving, and it's going way too fast. We'll be killed!"

"Not when I apply the emergency brake. I'm going to do it here, on the bend." Max showed Kensy and Curtis the map on his phone. "The train will have slowed already and, with the brake on, it should almost come to a stop."

"You never said that we were going to jump off a moving train," Curtis said, biting his lip.

Kensy turned to him. "You don't have to come. You can move to another car and pretend you don't know us. Although I'm not sure what sort of secret agent you can call yourself if you're not prepared to take the leap of faith," she said, knowing full well that Curtis would hate her saying that.

The boy licked his lips nervously. He knew watching all those martial arts videos online would come in handy. Just last week he'd been practicing his commando rolls at the park. The children watched as the ground sped past them.

"I'll do it," Curtis said with a gulp.

Kensy smiled and gave his shoulder a reassuring squeeze. "Good man."

"Almost there," Max said as the three of them stood by the door. At least it looked like they would be landing on soft ground – there hadn't been too many rocks since Moss Vale. Max pulled the lever and the brakes screeched. "Now!"

Kensy leapt off first. She tumbled along the grass and dirt, then scrabbled to her feet. "Come on, Curtis!" she yelled.

"I can't believe I'm doing this, but here goes!" The boy clamped his eyes shut and jumped out of the train. He rolled over and over, coming to a stop in a clump of wet manure. Thankfully, he didn't take too long to catch his breath, but his mother would be none too pleased with the stain on his jacket.

"Max, go!" Kensy shouted as she spied a guard running through from the car behind.

Max backed up, then put his head down and sprinted toward the door, his arms spinning like windmills in the air, before he landed with a thud on his feet.

"I'm calling the police, you little brats!" the guard shouted above the squealing brakes. The train had almost completely stopped, but Kensy, Max and Curtis had already set off through the thick stand of trees and into the fading light. A loud crack of thunder rumbled overhead and lightning split the sky. The children ran on, their feet flying over the dry ground. Kensy was gladder than ever that she'd worn her boots instead of those silly pumps Song had wanted her to buy.

"There, Max! There's the shed," she said as they drew closer. The building was surrounded by a high hedge and hidden below was a fence topped with barbed wire.

"What is this place?" Curtis asked.

"I told you – no questions," Kensy said. "Just trust us and do as we say."

Kensy and Max decided to scout the perimeter. They rounded the corner and spotted Dash's car and a white pickup.

"How are we going to get in?" Max said.

But it was Curtis who saw it first. There was a gate in the fence and it was open. The door to the shed was too. "Not as hard as you thought, maybe," the boy said.

"You stay here," Kensy ordered. "If we're not back in half an hour, go to the nearest house – no, not the nearest one, the next one after that – and call the police."

Curtis nodded. He still had no idea what the Greys were up to, but if that was his role, that's what he would do. "Max, take this," he said, offering his backpack.

Max grinned tightly. "Thanks."

Thick, fat drops rained down from the sky as thunder rumbled louder and closer until it collided with a lightning strike that shook the ground. Curtis jumped into the air, then ran and hid behind Dash Chalmers' car, out of sight.

Kensy and Max entered the building. There were a couple of tractors and various machines at one end, and at the other was what looked to be an office. The twins scurried toward it. Max poked his head around the open door and was surprised to see a heavy metal trapdoor in the floor. He tried to lift it by the handle, but it was firmly secured.

"It's a bunker," Kensy whispered. "There must be a ventilation shaft somewhere."

Max nodded. He crept back to the main part of the shed and shone Curtis's flashlight under the largest of the tractors before he found what he was looking for. "There!"

But the vent was covered by a grate. Fortunately, Curtis's Swiss Army knife had myriad screwdrivers, and within a few minutes the children had pried it free. Max shone the flashlight into the cylinder. It looked to go straight for a little way then turned at an angle. They needed the rope.

Kensy secured the end to the tractor suspension and dropped it into the hole, then lowered herself down. Max took a deep breath and followed suit. Outside, thunder boomed and lightning crashed.

Above the noise, Curtis heard a car approaching. He stole a peek and recognized it as the silver Mazda he'd taken down the license plate for the other day. The driver was the man who'd been snapping pictures of Van and Ellery. There was a woman with him too, but all Curtis could make out was her blonde hair. They parked behind a tree but didn't get out. Curtis had no idea what they were doing there, but he wasn't about to show himself. He needed to stay focused – if whatever the twins were doing went horribly wrong, someone had to be able to get help.

CHAPTER 40

ULFMW

Kensy realized too late that the rope wasn't long enough. She dropped the last few feet, causing a huge bang, which coincided perfectly with a booming clap of thunder. Her feet plummeted through a grate and onto something soft and completely unexpected – a couch.

Max landed beside her. "What is this place?" he whispered, looking around at what appeared to be some sort of living quarters. There was a kitchen in the corner and another room off to the right.

"Hector, is that you?" a woman called from the other room.

The twins froze as a slim woman with clear blue eyes and fine features opened the door and startled at the sight of the two children in front of her. For a moment nobody said a thing.

"Am I dreaming or are there really two children standing before me?" she said.

Hector Clement appeared through another door. He was shorter and broad shouldered with a full gray beard and gray hair several shades darker than the woman's. He walked to his wife's side and peered at the twins, wondering if, after over a decade in captivity, he had finally begun to hallucinate.

Kensington couldn't help thinking the woman's resemblance to their mother was striking.

For once it was Max who spoke first. "My name is Maxim Val d'Isère Grey – no, Spencer – and this is my twin sister, Kensington Méribel Spencer."

Marisol's face drained of color and

she looked as if she was going to pass out. She reached for her husband's arm to steady herself.

"You are Anna and Edward's children?" Hector said.

Kensy and Max nodded. "We've come to take you home, Grand-mère and Grand-père," the boy said.

"Mum and Dad have been looking for you for months," Kensy added.

Marisol's eyes filled with tears. "Oh my word."

"They are here too?" Hector asked.

Kensy shook her head. "No."

Marisol's breath caught in her throat and she crossed her hands on her chest. "Is this real, Hector? Am I dreaming?" Tears slid down her cheeks.

"We're real, Grand-mère," Kensy said, smiling through her tears.

Marisol opened her arms and pulled the twins into her embrace. Hector enveloped them all. For more than a minute they stood together, weeping.

"We've got to go," Kensy said eventually, wiping at her eyes.

Hector shook his head. "There is no way out of this place. Believe me, we have tried."

"There has to be," Max said. "Someone put you in here and now we're going to get you out."

* * *

There was a loud *whoosh* as the trapdoor opened and Dash climbed up the ladder with Nick behind him. Both men were carrying a biohazard box in one hand.

"I don't understand how the transport was canceled," Dash said. "Lucy had it all organized. She's never messed up a transfer."

Nick shrugged. "I was waiting for ages. When I called the number she'd given me, it said it was disconnected."

Dash tried to phone his assistant for the umpteenth time since leaving the city, but she wasn't picking up. The woman had been absolutely devoted to him for the past ten years and he couldn't remember there ever being a time she didn't take his calls, no matter the hour. This didn't make sense at all. "I'll have to get these to the plane myself or we'll miss the connections," he said, hefting the large biohazard case onto the floor.

"There are four more," Nick said. "I'll bring them up."

Dash glanced at the man's arm. "You know Tinsley's on to you."

"What do you mean?"

Dash chuckled. "She saw the scratch and thinks it was you who carjacked her, but don't worry, I've spoken to the police commissioner and you're in the clear. You'll have to be more careful next time."

"Next time?" Nick repeated.

"Only if she starts acting up again." Dash glanced at his watch. "Hurry, I'll put this in the car."

Dash picked up the two cases and walked out of the office into the shed. The door had blown shut in the wind. He kicked it open and hurried outside. The large spats of rain were coming down harder and faster. Dash charged around to the back of the four-wheel drive and pulled open the door.

Curtis had just enough time to get out of the way. He pressed himself against the back tire on the left-hand side and hoped that Dash wasn't about to drive off. His heart was pounding so loudly it was a wonder the man couldn't hear it over the crashing storm.

CHAPTER 41

UIVV

"How do they get things in and out of the lab?" Kensy asked.

Hector showed her the device which served as a dumbwaiter, sliding back and forth through the wall.

"I think I can fit in there," Kensy said.

Max shook his head. "What if it's sealed on the other side?"

"We have to try," Kensy said. She wasn't relishing the thought of tucking herself into a ball and being pushed through a thick concrete wall, but there was no other way.

Marisol clutched the girl's arm. "No, you mustn't go," she said vehemently. "They will kill you."

"I have to," Kensy said. She looked to Max for support. The boy took his grandmother's hand in his and squeezed it.

"Good luck, *ma chérie*," Marisol whispered, and kissed Kensy's forehead.

Kensy flicked on her flashlight as the box moved slowly toward its destination. If there was anyone waiting for her on the other side she was in big trouble, but to her surprise the panel slid up and she found herself in what looked like a control room.

Kensy unfurled herself and stared at a large screen. She studied the diagram and hoped with every fiber of her being that she was about to make the right choice. Her finger hovered over the green button for a moment, then she bit the bullet and pressed it. Seconds later, a panel slid away and she came face-to-face with her grandparents and Max.

"Come on!" Kensy hissed as they rushed

through. She flew up the ladder and through an open trapdoor with the others behind her, then came to a screeching halt at the top. "Nick," she breathed.

The man looked at her in surprise. "What are you doing here?" he demanded. "How did you get in?"

"You know you work for a monster," Kensy said. She hopped off the top rung and slowly walked toward the man.

"Turn around and go back downstairs," Nick ordered. "NOW!"

Kensy inched along the wall of the office, trying to distract him. Out of the corner of her eye, she saw Max hop over the top of the ladder too and then her grandparents. "I'm not going anywhere, but you will be — straight to prison when the police arrive."

Nick lunged at the girl, but Max was ready. He charged at the man, sending him sideways. Hector grabbed Marisol's hand and the two of them scurried across the room as Kensy spun around and landed a heavy kick to Nick's stomach. She lined up for another, except this time he managed to grab her by the foot and fling her away.

"Kensy!" Max yelled, running to his sister's aid. He delivered a blow to Nick's kneecap, aggravating an old football injury, which had the man moaning in agony. Max looked for something to defend himself. He spotted an open toolbox, but before he could reach it, Nick grabbed Max's leg and began pulling him toward the trapdoor.

"Oh, no, you don't," Max said, suddenly remembering his glasses. He pressed the logo on the side and a reticle appeared on the lens in front of his left eye. He zeroed in on Nick with the crosshairs and pressed the logo again, this time firing a tiny poison dart straight into the man's neck.

"Ow!" Nick swatted at the microscopic device, but the effects were immediate. He stood up and staggered forward until he fell through the open hatch and onto the concrete floor below.

"Oh my word." Marisol's eyes were huge as she watched her grandchildren in action.

Kensy looked at the two biohazard cases near the door. "What about these?"

"Bring them with us," Hector said. "But be very careful."

"Quickly, someone's coming," Max said. He guided Kensy and his grandparents to the other end of the shed. It was Dash, returning to collect the next two cases. He soon realized they weren't there.

"Nick! Hurry up. I've got to meet the plane in thirty minutes," he shouted.

Hector, Marisol and the twins were hiding behind a tractor. Who knew what Dash might do when he worked out what had happened?

Outside, Curtis hadn't dared to move. He was soaked to the bone, his hair plastered across his face. He poked his head out around the back of the car and was shocked to see the man from the ferry and the blonde woman were making a run for the shed.

"Nick! Where are you?" Dash peered into the opening and recoiled when he saw the man lying unconscious at the bottom. He looked around in confusion, then scampered down the ladder and grabbed another container. He didn't stop to check if Nick was still alive – there were far more important things on his mind.

"Hello?" a woman's voice echoed through the shed.

"Lucy! What are you doing here and why haven't you been answering your phone?" Dash demanded, as he exited the office with the case.

"Who's that?" Kensy whispered.

Max peered out just far enough to see that it was Dash's assistant. But then he spotted the man from the ferry lurking in the shadows, out of sight, with something in his hand. "It's Lucy," Max whispered, "and that journalist, George Kapalos."

"I need to ask you something," Lucy said, her voice wavering.

"What?" Dash roared. A huge clap of thunder shook the building. Rain hammered the tin roof.

"What is it that I've been organizing the transport for all this time?" she yelled.

"For heaven's sake, not now, Lucy. I'm in a hurry. Your mess up has meant I need to get this batch to the plane," Dash shouted.

"This isn't a vaccine, is it?" she pressed, marching into his path. Her hands were balled into two tight fists and her body was so tense it felt like it could snap at any second. "I know what you're doing, and it has to stop."

Dash scoffed. "I'm saving millions of people, that's what I'm doing."

Max peered around the tire again and realized that George Kapalos had a phone out, filming the exchange.

"You make people sick," Lucy hissed. "You spread the diseases then you make millions from the cures."

Max turned to his grandparents. "Is that true?"

Hector nodded.

"You're delusional, Lucy. Did you take a bump to the head?" Dash shouted.

Max hesitated for a second then stood up.

"What are you doing?" Kensy grabbed at his trousers, but he was too quick.

"She's telling the truth," Max said loudly as he emerged from his hiding spot.

Lucy flinched in fright and Dash did a double take. "Max?" he balked. "What are you doing here?"

Kensy appeared too, followed by Hector and Marisol.

Dash dropped the biohazard case in his hands. "How on earth did you . . .?"

"So, it was you," Hector said. "You have been our captor for these past twelve years."

Marisol clung to her husband's arm, shaking.

"Might you at least have the decency to tell us your name?" Hector said.

Lucy's jaw gaped open. She had no idea who these people were, but her boss had clearly done something even more despicable than she had uncovered.

"He's Dash Chalmers," Kensy said. "Head of The Chalmers Corporation."

At the revelation of the man's name, Hector staggered. "Your parents are Faye and Conrad Chalmers?"

"Do you know them?" Kensy asked. It was her turn to be confused.

Marisol nodded. "We were in talks to do business with them when we were taken. Their reputation is impeccable, but we never met their son."

"I don't have time for this," Dash said. He picked up the case and looked set to make a run for it. "If it makes you feel better, my parents don't know a thing."

"But why do it in the first place?" Hector breathed.

"Are you kidding?" Dash retorted. "You had developed a vaccine that would rid the world of every strain of the common cold. We would have lost everything going into business with you. I couldn't let them do it. This way, the company made billions."

Hector shook his head. "Thousands of innocent people suffered and many have likely died because of you and your greed."

"Collateral damage, old man," Dash sneered. "Now, get out of my way."

"You're not going anywhere." George Kapalos stepped into the light. "Except to prison. We have enough evidence to put you away for the rest of your sorry life."

Dash frowned. "Who are you?"

"He's a journalist who's been helping me with the paper trail, uncovering exactly what you've been up to all this time," Lucy said. She took a few steps toward him. "Tinsley's gone, Dash, and she's taken Van and Ellery with her. You'll never find them."

"What are you talking about? What have you done?" the man spat. "My wife is at home with our children – exactly where she belongs. She knows better than to try to leave me."

"Someone sent her a letter about your sister and how she died. Tinsley said that she couldn't stay with you any longer. She and the children weren't safe," Lucy retorted.

"Lies! It's all lies!" Dash looked at the box in his hands. He placed it on the ground and unlatched the clips, then reached in and pulled out a vial. "If any of you dare to come closer, I will break this and we will all be dead within a week."

"No! Don't you dare!" Hector yelled. "It cannot end this way."

"Clear a path for me to get to my vehicle and I will let you live," Dash said evenly.

Lucy stepped aside and George did too. Hector pulled Marisol back, shielding her.

The man edged past them. When he neared the door, he turned, his eyes full of venom. "Catch!" he shouted, and launched the vial high into the air, then fled into the storm.

The little glass container tumbled up and up and over and over.

Max sped toward it, but it was too far. Kensy spotted Curtis standing at the shed entrance and yelled, "Curtis! Catch it!"

The boy could see the object in the air. A flashback to last year's C-grade cricket final began to enter his mind, but he pushed it away. This time he wasn't going to drop the ball. His eyes never left the tube as he reached out. To everyone's great relief, it landed safely in his hands.

"Well done!" Hector shouted. "Now, hold it very carefully."

But the distraction had given Dash more than enough time. He was already in the car, its wheels spinning.

"He's getting away!" Lucy yelled as she, George and the twins charged out after him.

They could see Dash's taillights melting red in the pouring rain as the car rocketed down the sodden track, skidding and sliding. George ran toward his car, but a branch had come down in the storm, blocking it in. Meanwhile, inside the shed, Curtis had returned the vial to the box and secured the locks.

"Excuse me," Curtis said to Hector and Marisol, "I think I should go and help my friends." He ran outside to join Kensy and Max. The rain had stopped and all around them steam was rising from the earth.

Kensy threw her arms around the boy. "You were brilliant, Curtis, and your timing couldn't have been better."

"I heard lots of angry shouting and thought I'd take a look, in case you needed me." He shrugged. "Don't worry, I was ready to run as well."

"But we lost Dash. He'll be heading for the plane," Lucy said. "With his evil cargo."

"He doesn't have it," Curtis said. "I took out the boxes and hid them behind a tree."

Just as the children were about to retrieve them, they were stunned to see headlights on the driveway. Moments later, Song and Rupert leapt out of a silver sedan.

"Where is he?" Rupert demanded.

Kensy gasped. "Uncle Rupert, what are you doing here?"

"No time to explain. Where's Dash?" the man said desperately. He had a wild look about him, as if he hadn't slept in days.

"He got away," Max said. "He's heading for an airstrip."

"Where?" Rupert pleaded.

"I know," Lucy said. "I can take you there."

Rupert jumped back into the driver's seat. "Quick, get in!" he yelled out the window.

"I'm coming too," George said, making a run for the sedan. "I'll call the police on the way."

"No police," Lucy said. "He has everyone in his back pocket, right up to the commissioner."

"Uncle Rupert, how did you know?" Kensy cried out, but the man was already gone.

Song ran toward the children. "Are you all right? He didn't hurt you, did he?"

"We're fine," Max said. "We're all fine."

Song looked up and caught sight of Hector and Marisol standing by the shed door, instantly recognizing them from the handful of occasions they had attended family events at Alexandria. He rushed toward them. "Are my eyes deceiving me?"

"Dear Song." Marisol kissed the man on both cheeks and hugged him fiercely.

"Excuse me, I have a question," Curtis said, putting up his hand. Everyone turned to look at the boy. "Who are you all?"

Max grinned at his sister. "That's probably a story for another time."

Curtis sighed. "No, you need to tell me – who are you really?"

"Let's just say, Curtis," Kensy said, throwing an arm around his shoulder, "that one day, when you least expect it, you might get a call and all your wildest dreams will come true."

"I still don't understand," the boy said, shaking his head. "But I'm really glad you're my friends, because you're kind of scary – in a good way, I think." Curtis checked his watch. "Oh no, is that the time? Do you think we could go home soon? Mum's doing spaghetti Bolognese for dinner and it's my favorite."

"Home," Marisol said with tears in her eyes. She squeezed Hector's hand and gazed at her grandchildren. "What a wonderful notion."

CHAPTER 42

SLNV

After a hearty breakfast, the furthest the twins and their grandparents had moved was from the kitchen to the couch in the family room, where Hector had promptly sat on the stray ninja star Kensy had forgotten about from their training the other day. Max had quickly snatched it away, mumbling something about not knowing where on earth that could have come from. Before Hector and Marisol had come downstairs, Song had gently reminded the children that their grandparents had no knowledge of Pharos and for now it had to stay that way.

"Mum looks a lot like you," Kensy said to her grandmother. "You have the same nose and eyes."

Hector smiled. "Your mother is a great beauty, like your grandmother."

"And Anna is very clever, like her father," Marisol said, looking at her husband.

Kensy grinned. "That's just like us. Max is pretty and I'm smart."

"You don't know what you're talking about, Kens. I'm pretty *and* smart." Max rolled his eyes and his grandparents chuckled.

Marisol patted her granddaughter's hand. "I see you two have a wonderful rapport."

"Most of the time," Kensy said, squeezing the woman's hand in return. She didn't ever want to let it go.

Max curled his legs up on the couch opposite his grandmother and sister. "I still can't believe Dash Chalmers had you captive for twelve years. That's the whole of our lives and a little bit more."

"When you spoke his name, I was in shock," Hector said, shaking his head. "We had been in discussions with his parents on a project that would have changed the world."

Marisol's blue eyes hardened. "That man needs to be caught and brought to justice, and I hope with all my heart that his parents had no idea what he was up to."

"Don't worry, Uncle Rupert seemed pretty determined," Max said, though he and Kensy were still completely in the dark as to why the man was there in the first place and whether or not he'd managed to capture Dash Chalmers.

As for Nick, Song and the children had imprisoned the man in Hector and Marisol's apartment until Pharos could determine what they would do with him. They could afford to take their time as he had enough supplies to survive for months. All things considered, the twins felt as if their mission was like a giant jigsaw puzzle that was still missing several important pieces.

"Would anyone care for a piece of cake?" Song asked.

"Yes, please," a voice called from the front hall.

"Fitz!" Kensy and Max charged down the short flight of steps to the lounge. "We did it! We found them!" they said, jumping about excitedly.

Fitz stepped back and grinned. "Amazing job, kids."

Kensy peered over his shoulder, a worried look on her face. "But . . ."

"I did it too, Kens," Fitz said as the door pushed open and Anna and Edward Grey walked inside.

"Mum! Dad!" the children exclaimed, rushing into their parents' embrace.

"You two are a sight for sore eyes," Ed said, smiling from ear to ear. "We're so proud of you both."

"I can't believe you found them," Anna said, her eyes brimming with tears. She looked up and gasped. "Maman, Papa." She clasped her hands to her mouth and ran to her parents.

Amid the weeping and hugging, there was simply nothing to say – for the moment. Hector and Marisol greeted their son-in-law, but when it came to Fitz, Marisol faltered.

"Fitzgerald," she said, "is that really you?"

"He's let himself go, hasn't he?" Ed teased, and the twins giggled.

"My dearest Marisol, I can assure you, I will be back to my old self in no time flat," Fitz said. He cast a worried glance at the butler. "Won't I, Song?"

"Of course, sir." Song picked up the small bottle of solvent from the kitchen counter and waved it about a little too enthusiastically. It slipped from his grasp and flew into the air. Max was under it like a shot. He dove and caught it inches from the floor.

"Great job, Max!" Ed cheered.

Max stood up and passed the bottle to Fitz.

"Thanks, mate," the man said, breathing a sigh of relief. "You know you might just make a champion slips fielder yet."

"Has anyone told my mother the good news?" Ed asked.

Max shook his head, a twinkle in his eye. "We were waiting for you," he said. Then, lowering his voice, added, "Is this the end of our time with Pharos?"

"On the contrary, I suspect you and your sister are only just getting started," Ed replied with a wink.

Max grinned and Kensy beamed at her parents. "We've got so much to tell you," she gushed.

"It's going to take days – no, weeks – to catch you up on everything," Max said, his eyes widening. "Maybe even months."

Anna laughed. "Take as long as you need, my darlings. We've got all the time in the world."

THE ATBASH CIPHER

Originally a monoalphabetic cipher used for the Hebrew alphabet, the Atbash cipher is one of the earliest and simplest substitution ciphers to have been devised. The cipher simply reverses the plaintext alphabet to create a ciphertext alphabet. For example, the first letter of the alphabet, A, is encrypted to the last letter of the alphabet, Z. B becomes Y, C becomes X and so forth.

A	B	C	D	E	F	G	H	I	J	K	L	M	N	O	P	Q	R	S	T	U	V	W	X	Y	Z
Z	Y	X	W	V	U	T	S	R	Q	P	O	N	M	L	K	J	I	H	G	F	E	D	C	B	A

While not considered a strong cipher, it still provides an easy way to conceal messages and can be made more difficult by adding ten digits at the end along with commonly used punctuation.

	.	,	?	!	A	B	C	D	E	F	G	H	I	J	K	L	M	N	O	P
9	8	7	6	5	4	3	2	1	0	Z	Y	X	W	V	U	T	S	R	Q	P

Q	R	S	T	U	V	W	X	Y	Z	0	1	2	3	4	5	6	7	8	9
O	N	M	L	K	J	I	H	G	F	E	D	C	B	A	!	?	,	.	

Ready to do some spy work of your own? Using the key on the previous page, try your hand at decoding the chapter headings in this book. Good luck!

ABOUT
THE AUTHOR

Jacqueline Harvey taught for many years in girls' boarding schools. She is the author of the bestselling Alice-Miranda series and the Clementine Rose series, and was awarded Honor Book in the 2006 Australian CBC Awards for her picture book *The Sound of the Sea*. She now writes full time and is working on more Alice-Miranda, Clementine Rose, and Kensy and Max adventures.

jacquelineharvey.com.au

Read Them All!